into the madness

A.K. KOONCE

To every good person out there who's just a little bit bad. Embrace that villainous.

Table of Contents

Chapter One

*H*ere's the thing, I make really shitty decisions. I know I'm making them, and yet, I follow through with them anyway because, if I'm going to fuck something up, I should do it properly, right?

Yes, I'm the queen of bad choices. Take right now for example.

"Ah, fuck, Madison." His dick grinds against my thigh in a sensation of smooth and hard all at the same time.

It'd be sexy if the guy had a clue where my vagina was.

"Can you just"—I shift in frustration against him, and it only makes him groan more—"no, that's…my hip not my clit. Austin, stop rubbing it, it's not a magic lamp."

"Dallas. My name's Dallas," he says, his heavy breath tinged with beer fanning across my breasts.

"Right. I knew it was something about Texas."

"What?" His eyes flutter closed when he thrusts into the apex of my thigh, and I glare at him when his body suddenly goes completely still.

Silence cuts in.

And warmth starts to trickle down my leg.

What the literal fuck.

"Did you just…" My jaw clenches, and I can't even say it.

He fucked my leg.

I wanted to lose *my* virginity; I wanted this one thing to cross off my bucket list after the absolute worst year of my life, and this asshole tried to give my hip an orgasm.

And failed.

"Did you come?" He looks to me with the most hope-filled blue eyes.

He's kind looking with dark square glasses. A little on the nerdy side. That's why I picked him at the Alpha Phi Halloween party. So, I took two tequila shots, then I led him out to a *mostly* secluded, *hardly* romantic tree and prepared to finally do one thing right. I thought he'd be one of those guys who takes care of a girl in every way.

Instead I get the most cringeworthy question.

Did. I. Come?

Something in me snaps. It splinters down the center, and all that positive energy I've clung to for the past three years breaks away.

"You mean when you fucked two inches to the left of my vag for approximately thirty seconds? No. No, I didn't fucking come, Tex." I shove out of his arms, and the warm feeling that was trailing down my thigh is now cold and disgusting feeling.

Just like me.

"It's Dallas." Once again, his name doesn't register in my mind for some reason. Maybe I just want to forget him already.

"Come on. I thought you were a nice girl. Don't be a bitch."

And there it is: I'm a nice girl.

Who's really just a bitch.

Usually when guys say that, they're wrong. For once, someone got it right.

I weave through the crowded party. Drunken coeds laugh a bit too loudly, and as hard as I try, I'm still an outsider looking in. Moving from Chicago to Southern California was a change of scenery, but it doesn't change me.

It doesn't change my past.

Sure, I'm no longer the Sick Girl like everyone affectionately called me in high school. Even after I beat leukemia. That name was a tag on who I was as a person. I'm not that person any more. I'm not that overly optimistic little girl trying to hang on a little longer for her mother.

There's no one to force a brave face for anymore.

My mom's gone.

But my cancer's back.

I think the bad news Dr. Dusk gave me last month after two years of remission is eating away at me more than the actual sickness is. I can't fake a good attitude on my own.

How am I supposed to do this on my own?

"Alice," a guy with white rabbit ears says and slides his hand around my waist, pressing me into his side until my blue dress wrinkles against his black vest. "In Wonderland, Alice is shown around by a hare, if I remember right."

His costume doesn't say Wonderland at all. It was a story my mother read to me thousands of times. I know Wonderland. His generic white ears are a lazy excuse for a costume.

I made this pale blue dress myself, borrowed my roommate's blonde wig, found a black headband, and legitimately want-ed to have a good time tonight. I wanted to find some happiness.

I need to find happiness. Positivity is crucial for me right now.

Bitterness is just so much easier.

I slip out of his arms and grab a fistful of white napkins. I make to leave but then double back through the backyard and steal another bottle of wine before sneaking down to the dark beach. It's empty. The party at the beach house on the hill leaves faint beats of music and trickling laughter in the air. The crash of the white waves almost drowns it out though.

Before I moved here, I had no idea the ocean had a sound. I always imagined the white drifting light the moon would cast across the sea, but I never really thought about how demanding and consuming the waves sounded.

It's calming. This is good. This inspires happiness.

For the moment.

My hand pushes the napkins quickly down my thighs, and I force myself not to think about Houston ever again. Starting now.

I twist the top of the bottle and tip my head back to take the largest drink I can.

Wine. Wine will make me happy.

Closer and closer, I inch toward the water until I'm stand-ing knee deep in the forceful pushing waves. My balance wavers, but more and more drinks from the bottle seem to keep me re-silient against the strength of the ocean. Or maybe the wine just takes away my ability to care.

Probably that second one. White water collapses over my white knee-high socks and thighs, making me stumble back. It trails out into the inky depths as quickly as it came.

4

Being here feels reckless and relaxing all at the same time.

The waves rise the longer I stand here until the ends of my dress that I worked so hard on become damp and cold.

Once more, the water tears up toward the coast with vengeance. This time when I stagger, laughter tumbles out as well with a feeling of freedom, peace.

Happiness.

Salt is all I smell. Clean, pure salt. I lean into that addicting calmness the ocean offers, the water up to my waist now, my big green eyes reflecting in the dark water for only an instant.

The crash of it all, that's the serene part. The roaring, intense, violence of the water is absolutely beautiful.

It almost smothers the sound of my scream when it all happens.

A hand grips my arm, wrapping cold fingers around my skin until I feel it in my bones even. Ink scars the fingers that dig into my flesh. A mixture of pale skin and black lines make up every inch of the hand emerging from the waves.

A strangled sound of fear claws up my throat, but it's silenced in an instant.

It's silenced as I go under. The beautiful waves that I admired so much take away every sound of my fear. A coldness surrounds me, drenching my pretty blue dress and stark white socks as I'm pulled deeper and deeper into the darkness.

I came to Los Angeles to escape. Maybe I should've been careful what I asked for.

Chapter Two

Salt stings my throat, and I gasp for a steady breath of air when I cough it up. My hands fist damp sand, and my chest aches as I kneel on all fours, ready to sacrifice my right lung for a decent breath of air. Warm fingers run up and down my spine.

"You're all right. Cough it up, Prospect." The even tone of his low voice hums along the sound of the slashing waves. The beautiful sound of the sea is oddly dull compared to the deep rumble of his voice.

My lashes flutter, and I manage to look at the man by my side. For a moment, I expect to see Tex. It's a stupid moment, I'll admit. If he can't find my pussy when it's pressed right up against him, there's no way he's going to find my entire body in the Pacific Ocean.

Only the moonlight gives me glimpses of his appearance. Water drips from the ends of the stranger's light hair. Blue searching eyes follow my every motion. Pale hair, pale eyes, pale skin, and black inking lines that slash across nearly every inch of him.

They're…numbers. Numbers and dates and hyphens in some places. His right arm rests against his knee as he crouches at my side. Dark Roman numerals, romantic swirling dates, and quickly jotted numbers etch up his arms. The tattoos scar his knuckles, along the insides of his fingers, over every inch of him but his untouched face.

And I can see why.

There's strength in the line of his jaw. Perfect full lips are set into an emotionless line. Piercing blue eyes watch me watching him.

He's fucking beautiful. I traveled the country after high school, and I never saw anyone as perfectly made as this man.

He saved me.

"Clear your lungs, Prospect. We have a long trip ahead of us. We can't be late." He stands, his gaze colliding with the sea.

Sand sprinkles across his black boots, and I try to peer up at his towering height as I all but slouch into the sand like a crab ready to hibernate.

I appreciate his heroism. I do. Really. But I'm fine right here where I am. Let me hack up a lung in peace.

My eyes close slowly. It's then that I realize the pounding music of the party is no longer ripping through the night air.

I take a time out from dying slowly to process that.

My lashes open. I take in the heavy waves lapping at the rocky shore. The sand beneath my palms is as smooth and silky as ever. I shift ungracefully to look back at the scenery behind me. The overwhelming structure of the enormous beach house is no longer there.

Dark trees and twisting vines are everywhere. They wrap around for miles and miles. The sea is ahead while a tropical forest is behind.

And only my heroic friend is here.

Alone.

Shit. I'm alone with a man who may or may not be a friend. I've basically already idolized him for saving me. Let's face it, a woman who's spent half her life isolated from her peers knows Stockholm syndrome when she falls face fucking first into it.

And now we're alone, my savior and I.

On shaking legs, I stand. Sand scrapes through my hair as I attempt to smooth my wig back into place. The clips pull against my scalp, and I wince instantly. I take a step back. And then another. And another.

"I actually have to go. My friends are waiting for me." Friends. That's good. Good job, Maddy. "My boyfriend gets really angry when he has to wait for me." Oh yes. The boyfriend. The *angry* boyfriend. I'm just about to toss out more scary words for the man who may be a hero, or he may be a future homicidal maniac who just happens to like women in dripping mascara and crooked wigs, when he says something I never could have expected.

"Wanderlust is expecting you. This is In Trance Island, and there's only one exit, I'm afraid." His tone is this alluring sound that only better confirms that he's a murderer. They're charming, you know. Charming and alluring and they say charismatic things like *there's only one exit.*

"*Entrance Island?*" I ask.

A killer—murderous—smile almost slips over the hard line against his lips.

"Not quite."

With a single step, he covers the space between us, and I stumble against the soft sand to put more distance in place.

"In Trance." The rasping whisper of his words seems to stir something within the island itself. Shimmering fog in shades

of pink and purple pools around our legs. Fear pushes against my chest, and I can't help but breathe it all in, all the pretty colors.

I must look like a weak little sheep ready for slaughter.

But my instincts are screaming a totally different appearance.

I look up at the handsome stranger one last time.

And then I run.

On unsteady steps, I tear through the lashing forest on black high heels that I'm now regretting. I kick them off and keep going. Vines and limbs snap against my skin, and still I claw my way into the darkness. The moonlight is repressed from the twisting limbs above. The only light is the glimmering colors of the fog that's creeping higher and higher and higher. I stumble here and there. I never stop running.

Even as the whispers in the shadows start to talk to themselves and become unbearably louder.

"She's here."

"She's there."

"She's *nowhere*."

"Is she royal or is she mad?"

"Either way, both are bad."

"She's beautiful, exactly like they said."

"If she isn't careful, she'll soon be dead."

The eerie voices jolt terror into my bloodstream, distracting me the more they circle around the trees. They claw at me until I stumble. A cry of pain falls from my lips as my hands hit hard against the terrain. My fingers dig into the wet mud. My eyes open just as black boots interrupt the pink fog.

"You lost your heels, Prospect." Two black high heels slap against the puddle I'm resting in. My lungs ache as I realize I've put zero amount of space between myself and my heroic murderer. I'm not even going to be that woman that they say put up a good fight in the end.

They'll say he slathered Madison Torrent in mud and leaves to cover up the fact that she was a train wreck before he even captured her.

My lashes flutter slowly as I take another heaving breath of the pink wafting fog.

His movements are drifting and delayed, and I can't seem to track them as I struggle to keep my eyes open. It's then that I realize how similar his eyes are to the glinting sea. The hypnotic water is what got me into this mess.

Now I'm staring mesmerized by that color all over again.

"Konstance will be displeased about the state of your appearance, Prospect. She likes the prospects to look a certain way. A hopeful way. A…you know, you'll have to do. It is what it is." He shakes his head at me in blurring movements.

All those crime shows I watched on repeat in the hospital drift through my thoughts. I should have spent my days binging *Jeopardy*, and maybe then I'd be smart enough to get out of this. Instead I'm analyzing everything my murderer does just before he does it. Watching those shows in chemo, I always said I'd never be the girl who didn't put up a fight.

I barely have the energy to reply.

My words are a slurred garble of sounds as I put the last strength I have into jerking my leg up hard between his thighs. He groans when my foot connects with his balls.

Once more, I mumble to him a ridiculous string of words that don't really make any sense in my mind.

"All I wanted was an orgasm."

His groan of pain is interrupted as confusion creases his

brow.

"Konstance is going to be so disappointed." He shakes his head and stands, adjusting himself with a wince.

My lashes become heavier. His arms slip around me, warming my body with his. The last thing I remember is burying my head into my sweet captor's chest.

And feeling completely calm at last.

Chapter Three

ater sloshes against my face. A rocking gentleness makes my stomach turn just slightly. Then my eyes find him. From above me, he sits with steely posture. His gaze rakes over the night, surveying every detail while the moon and stars highlight the tense set of his brow.

My fingers run over the smooth wooden floor just as his arms flex hard, and he maneuvers two oars simultaneously.

Because we're on a boat.

Pain stings my spine as I try to sit up from my humble little place on the floor of the damp rowboat. My legs tangle with the wooden board that acts as a makeshift bench. As I sit up, my forehead collides with the underside of the man's seat. His crotch is poised just above my face, and I grimace once more when my wincing gaze lingers there for a bit too long.

There's probably something in the *Surviving Murder* handbook about not looking at your captor's bulge for longer than five seconds. Or ten.

"Fuck." My fingertips skim over my temple as slicing pain

radiates there.

"You just keep getting better by the minute, Prospect."

I glare over at my captor and sloppily sit up. My heels stab against my own calves as I try to make it to a graceful sitting position in the little seat opposite of the man. Did he…put my shoes on me? Oh God, he's dressing me up now. My fingers shake against the slick warmth that's slipping down from my hairline. I wipe the blood away, nearly pushing off the wig entirely.

I try to make sense of everything. The pink fog. The tattooed man. The rowboat. What the fuck have I gotten myself into?

"Where are you taking me?" My attention shifts discreetly over the boards at my feet. There isn't anything. There's nothing but the oars to act as a weapon. And seeing how I'd be lost at sea, I should probably halt all of my escape plans until we hit the shore again.

"What's your name?" His gaze trails over every disorderly inch of my body.

"My name's Fuck You. Where are you taking me?"

"That's a pretty name, Fuck You. Not something I'd want to say as introduction to my mother, but it'd have a nice ring to it in bed, I suppose." There's no amusement in his features as he stares past me at the unending sea beyond. "My name's Kais St. Croix. I'll be your guide while in Wander. We are currently headed toward the Wanderlust Kingdom, the Kingdom of Hearts, as some like to call it. There we will meet with King Constantine, Konstance, the royal court, and of course the Profit."

The prophet, the royal court, King Constantine. These words pass over and over through my mind. Maybe this is just a drunken dream. I take another look at Kais's features. Could I dream up someone as uniquely perfect as him? My fingers press to the slick wound at my head. Pain stings there all over again. That feels real.

The pink fog. That couldn't be real. Could it?

"So I'm in Wanderlust?" The word feels odd against my tongue.

He nods without meeting my gaze and continues rowing. I try not to note how the muscles of his biceps constrict hard with every push against the sea. He looks like he's done this a time or two. I mean, looking at how big his arms are, I'd say he does this a few times a day, really.

Not that I've noticed. The Surviving Murder Association would be so damn disappointed in me. They are not going to re-new my membership next year if I keep it up.

He's frightening in a way. Beautiful and frightening. I pause just shortly to try to imagine him without the hundreds of tattoos that slink up underneath the short sleeves of his white t-shirt. I can't. I can't picture him without the lines that adorn his body. They only add to his menacing appearance.

"And I'll be presented to the King?"

Another nod.

"Will I be crowned?" My eyebrows raise as I try to consid-er just how elaborate I make my dreams nowadays. I can't decide if any minute now a unicorn will leap from the sea and make all my childhood fantasies come to life or if my teeth are all about to tum-ble randomly out of my mouth only for me to find myself standing toothless and nude in front of my high school crush.

He scoffs at the word *crowned*. The first glimpse of a real smile pulls at his lips.

"Doubtful. You're—" he glances down at the ink scrawl-ing across his arms and hands. "You're just another number, really. The odds of you being 'The One' are unlikely."

The One.

A frown pulls at my lips.

It's my dream, asshole. If I'm supposed to be *The One*, I

probably will be.

The sigh that forces from my lungs is more from agitation than exhaustion. I've been tired and exhausted since chemo started again, but I feel…different now. A bit more rejuvenated. Maybe nearly dying in the ocean will do that to a person. I don't know.

I can't understand anything.

My elbow rests against the hard edge of the boat, and I prop my chin against my hand as I stare out at the drifting sea. It's quiet but lapping. Constantly moving and yet, going nowhere.

"I wouldn't get too close." With a small lift of his chin, he gestures to the waters.

Glimmering flecks of gold shine within the sea. The moonlight plays against the beautiful glinting pieces. It paints it. The tiny hypnotic flecks paint the sea with sparkling light until I can see into the dark depths.

Movement glides through the water in sapphire colors of long limbs that I can't quite make out.

Water sprays. It flings up violently from the ocean. A long tentacle crawls from the sea and wraps around my wrist. A crushing grip pulls at my hand, and I can't stop the scream that tears up my throat. My nails claw at the tightening blue limb. In one hard pull, I'm jerked forward. My hand slips beneath the cold, glittering sea. Enormous watchful eyes meet mine from within the water. They narrow on me, the hold on my wrist turning unbearably painful. The force of the creature below pulls harder. It steals the breath right from my lungs as my nose skims the surface of the ocean.

It has me, and it isn't letting go.

Then a shining object slices through my line of sight. The sound of a blade striking wood thuds hard and jarring. The demanding grip of the tentacle loosens before the slimy limb slides right off my flesh and drops back into the water with a plop. I stare after the drifting and lifeless tentacle for several seconds as my hand rubs back and forth against my wrist.

"I told you not to get too close." The vacant, bored sound of Kais's voice pulls at my attention. I sit stiffly back into the center of the boat, careful to hold my hands to my chest as my wide gaze skims along the surface of the endless sea.

With care, he rips the blade from the side of the boat and places the sword behind him. The weapon is out of sight, but it's very much in mind.

In silence, I watch him row for miles and miles. Cool winds shift against his short blond hair. Chills shiver all through me, but I don't say another word.

He could have killed me while I slept, but he didn't. He's supposedly my guide. For the moment, I do need him. He said there's only one exit.

That is the real issue here.

"Where's the exit?" It's the first thing I've said to him in almost an hour. He saved my life—twice—but I just don't have any kindness to show him.

It's a conflicting arrangement we have. He stole me away, but he's also keeping me safe.

There's no trust between us. Even if he saved me a thousand times, he's always going to be my captor.

I've never known who I can trust. Not in college, not here. I guess growing up with people calling you Sick Girl makes you a little vehement toward others. It isn't my sweet murderer's fault I distrust him, but my outlook isn't going to change any time soon.

"The exit is through Dismay Forest in the Elders' Kingdom." His quick answer cuts through my dark thoughts.

There's no hesitation when he speaks. I ask and he answers. It's odd. If I am his captive, why would he feed me information

so freely? My mind takes in his confusing answer and demands another and another.

"What will the King do with me?"

"If you're Alice, he'll keep you. Crown you just like you wanted." His cold blue eyes meet mine for only a moment. The look in his eyes makes me think he's the kind of man who's been hardened by life. It's hurt him and it shows.

"And if I'm not Alice?"

"Then you're free to leave, Prospect."

"Why do you keep calling me that?"

"It sounds more appealing than Fuck You."

Damn. He's right. But the pettiness in me won't allow me to tell him that.

"And the Prophet, what will the Prophet do?"

That near smile tilts the corner of his lips again as he continues to row us into the distance. God, he's too attractive when he smiles. If sex had a poster child, it'd be Kais St. Croix. Coincidently, if America's Most Wanted had a poster child, it'd also be Kais St. Croix.

"The *Profit*," he enunciates that word in that deep delicious tone of his, but I'm not sure why, "will declare if you're you or not."

"If I'm not me, who else would I be?"

In an appreciating way, his gaze trails over my body slowly before coming back to meet my eyes.

I'm a fucking mess, so I don't have a clue what he sees in me.

"In Wanderlust, you can be anyone. You can be whatever your heart desires."

A strange feeling flares to life within me, making my heart

17

pound harder. No more Sick Girl. I can be anyone. I can be *someone*. Finally.

"Unless you're Alice."

"And then I'm destined to be the King's Queen."

He nods, a subtle movement of his head.

Hmmm…Alice is better than Sick Girl. Not that it matters. I have leukemia. I wonder what their Prophet will say about that.

"Why is Alice so important to the Prophet and the King?"

"The *Profit* has declared a woman of resilient strength, kindness, and intelligence to be the peace within the two Kingdoms. He says it'll end all the suffering of our people. Alice will be the final newcomer to this realm. Wanderlust was made for Alice." Kais pauses to do an inventory of all the bruises and scrapes I've done to myself since we've met.

I bet I look strong and smart, for sure.

I smooth a clump of mud off of my cotton skirt, and it hits the floor with a sloppy plopping sound.

Yeah, I'm definitely Alice material.

"Why do you think her name will be Alice?" I try my best to brush the random dried blood off my palm and find that a small cut slices down the center of it from my fall in the forest. A sharp breath sneaks in through my teeth as I press too hard on it.

"There are miscellaneous visions here and there. Little details that the Profit has collected over the centuries."

"*Centuries*." My voice cuts through his words as my eyes widen.

"We've been waiting a long time for the woman who calls herself Alice. Like I said, it's not likely that you're The One. You're more likely just another brick in the foundation of this world. We're all rather used to disappointment by now." His tone makes

it sound like he's only ever disappointed.

Me too, friend, me too.

I stare at him in silence. He avoids my gaze, so I take the moment to just openly study him.

He'd be really sexy if he smiled more. Dangerously sexy. Tattoos, strong body, deep eyes. My mother would be shooing him away with yesterday's newspaper if she ever set eyes on Kais St. Croix. My virginity on the other hand would be waving him down like a landing strip waiting for a fighter jet to soar right in.

"Don't look at me like that, Prospect." He keeps his attention on the sky, somber expression held in place as he keeps a steady pace rowing.

"Like what?" I fight the smile against my lips, trying hard to mimic his careless expressions.

He levels me with a gaze that pours right into me. "Just don't."

The small smile that wanted so badly to slip into place falls away entirely. He's too serious. He isn't playful. He's every bit as dangerous as I thought he was when we were on land.

I don't know why I'm trying to see him in a different light. Stockholm syndrome. Definitely Stockholm.

It's not like I trust him. He has a long way to go to find the trust that's somewhere sunken low and forgotten within me.

With another hard push of the oars through the sea, the boat lurches abruptly. My body shifts forward before rocking back. I look up just as he stands. Behind him, up the side of a cliff, high up in the heavens, twinkling lights dot the darkness. A warm golden glow splays around the small lights. There are only a few, maybe a dozen at the most, but they're a beautiful warm color against the stark dark setting.

A village with broken lamp lights and disorderly shack

homes stacked too closely together meets the coast. The lanes of the roads are jagged and carelessly bricked. The entire place looks dark and dirty.

The petite woman who crosses the street is what's truly unsettling. Her arms reach out for the door of a small house, and the lantern light above shines through the thin white wings on her back. Delicate features lead up to a hairless skull, and two long feathery antennae twitch atop her head.

She slips inside. I'm left gaping in horror at the sight of… the creature. The…moth woman.

Kais climbs out of the small boat with ease, pulling it harder into the sand, making me nearly fall to the floor once again. This time, I stay there for several seconds, my heart pounding, my body unable to move.

Kais seems completely unaware.

The edge of the blade scrapes against the old wood as he pulls it from the floor and slips it carefully into a belt at his hip.

He looks back at the twinkling lights above the cliff. With a snap of his fingers, beaming red embers flare from his fingertips, shooting up into the night sky. The firing color blooms out in waves, lighting up the night with this signal of crimson.

I look to Kais's palm, but nothing's there. No flare gun. No fireworks. Just him.

My spine stiffens when his cold gaze settles on me.

He tilts his head at me as if he's just noticing my unease. As if when I ran from him wasn't enough for him to know I don't trust him. But right now, now he sees my apprehension of this place.

This isn't a dream. It's a nightmare.

"It's Wanderlust." He hesitates, waiting for understanding to fall into place.

It doesn't.

"Wanderlust is like a feeling. But it's also a sort of magic this world gives us. The longer you're here, the more that magic settles into you."

"M-magic?"

I want to say more. I want to ask about the moth lady, but all I can manage are the uneven breaths that are falling from my lips.

He looks uncomfortable as he stands before me, and I sit gaping up at him. Fear trickles in slowly at first and then it crashes, pressing in on my chest and gripping my lungs.

A light flickers on from high above. It shines through a square window. Another lights up. Another and another and another. Until a daunting castle is outlined against the dark sky on the very edge of the cliff above.

It's then I realize his magic was a signal. He was signaling that I'm here. He notified the creatures of this land.

"Come. We don't want to be late." He extends a big hand to me.

A thousand thoughts fly through my mind. Every one of them is just as stupid and dangerous as the last. But one sticks out among all others.

I need to find Dismay Forest.

The boat shifts beneath me as I stand in my three-inch heels in the middle of the rickety little boat. His pale eyes skim up my dirty white socks over my long legs, torn dress, and tight material before meeting my gaze.

Does he see my intentions there? Does he know?

If I had to guess, I'd say no.

In one swift move, I grab the oar and fling it up with more strength than I've had in weeks. The impact of it against his jaw shakes through my hands hard enough for me to drop the thing. An angry curse growls through him. I leap, my heels sinking the moment I touch land.

And then I run.

Chapter Four

Sand slides within my shoes with every step I take on the beach. I never once look back. Not even when I enter the dark streets. The uneven cobblestone makes it impossible to run.

Not that I know where I'm going.

He said the exit was through the Dismay Forest though. I'll find it eventually. I just have to put distance between us. If I could find another woman, someone less creepy, a bit less intimidating, a tad fewer sexy tattoos, then I'll just ask for directions. Simple. I'm in a mysterious Kingdom filled with massive sea creatures, insect women, and magic, and I'm trying to find logic and reason somewhere in between.

Not a problem at all.

Look at me and all my positivity finally.

Gleaming violet eyes blink back at me from somewhere in the darkness. It's enough to make me stumble in my tracks. With my next staggering step, an uneven stone in the road hits my heel, and down I go. Pain stabs into my palms, and I search out the watchful eyes.

But they're gone.

Someone else steps into view though. Big legs lead up to a broad chest, and I'm so hopeful for someone I can trust, someone who can help me. Someone…with many, many thin arms reaching down for me. The man's touch is like crawling insects along my skin. His countless arms pull me against his big body, and he starts to drag me away into a side street.

My heels scrape against the stone, and I try to find my footing, I try to shove away from him, I try to bite, kick, scream, anything, but he's too strong. All those slender arms work together, and they crush me to him.

Bile stings my throat the next time I scream, and I see a lone abandoned building up ahead. It's dark and ominous, and it's most definitely the place he's taking me to.

I can't breathe. There's not a breath in my lungs, but I scream anyway.

I scream his name despite how much I swore I wouldn't trust him.

"Kais. Kais. FUCKING KAIS!"

My body jolts forward, the man covering me, slamming me to the ground hard as we both fall. A sharp cracking noise sounds through my head, and the weight pressing down on me is thrown to the side. Kais stands tall, looming over the man with death in his eyes as he glares down on him, his sword held firmly in hand. He arches it up and brings it down in one quick sweep of the blade.

A crying scream and chaotic flipping and flopping follows the slice of the sword. I peer over with disgust to find the man's many arms convulsing like erratic fish on the ground.

"Touch the King's property again, and I'll quarter you." Kais's jaw grinds shut, and he sheaths his weapon at his lean hips.

He really is making my demented affection for him worse and worse. Someone needs to slap the crazy out of me now before my irrational affection for this man gets any worse.

Too late.

The air knocks from my lungs. I'm tossed over his shoulder with ease, and I'm almost thankful to be carried away from whatever other creatures this village is hiding in its darkness.

Why am I so damn happy to be in my captor's arms? What in the *Law & Order: SVU* is wrong with me? I swear I was a logical woman before I met him.

The firmness of his ass is right in my face as my arms dangle pathetically over my head. Strong hands hold my thighs as he walks casually through the forest.

"You know, I think I misjudged you, Fuck You."

I roll my eyes at the name I gave myself and his unwillingness to forget it.

Why can't he be like me? I forget ninety-eight percent of names the moment they're spoken. But no, I give him a sarcastic name one time, and he refuses to let it go.

"Misjudged me how?" I peer down at the blade on his opposite hip as it shifts back and forth with his every step.

I'm not athletic. I'm that person whose arms get tired from holding her Kindle up for too many hours late into the night.

But I'm not the sort of person who gives up either.

"Maybe you are The One."

My eyes widen just slightly. My fingers open as I quietly extend my hand toward the hilt.

"You're definitely one big pain in my ass. Stop stretching,

you're never going to reach that, Prospect."

My jaw tightens as I meld against his back, fisting his shirt in my hand to try to grip the shining sword. It's a struggle, an embarrassing struggle that isn't getting me anywhere.

"As big of an asshole that he is, he's usually right," a smooth voice says from behind us.

My palm presses against his lower back—God, is every part of him hard as rock?—and I heave myself up to see the person. With my other hand, I shove the long blonde locks from my face. I feel like such a shit show right now. I look like a toddler being carried out of the grocery store mid-tantrum. I'm astounded the wig has held in place this well.

The brick roads are no longer beneath us, and dirt and leaves take their place. The scent of pine fills the air as our surroundings become a bit darker among the trees.

Shining violet eyes meet mine. I can't make out much of her features, but she seems to be a woman. What kind of terrifying woman, I don't know. The way she walks is a calm and smooth movement. It's like nothing in this world can get in her way. The slinking way she shifts through the trees captures my attention as she follows behind us.

"Another Alice?" she asks, her pretty eyes look up to the back of Kais's head.

"One more to add to the list." He keeps walking without pausing to see if our new friend is following. His steps become jarring, and I look down to find wooden steps beneath us. He pounds his boots against them without care, jolting my head against his lower back with every quick step he takes.

She's right; he is an asshole.

Can he be a savior and an asshole at the same time? Well, I'm a good person and also a bitch at the same time, so I guess anything's possible.

"I think you're hurting New Alice," the woman says.

"Temporary Alice can fend for herself."

"You think so? She looks so delicate. Breakable. Delicious." A long finger strokes along my cheek before I pull my face away from the woman's hand.

"You don't know Fuck You Alice like I do, Cat."

Oh my God. My name keeps getting worse and worse with each passing second.

Harder he stomps, making the weak boards groan beneath us. I mentally try to calculate how much weight he and I are putting on the thin boards. My hand presses against his ribs to better adjust myself, meeting nothing but hard muscle underneath. Shit, muscle weighs more than fat.

It's not looking good for us.

The dark forest slips away, and ocean breeze tangles my hair. I look down to see the crashing waves far below. The white water slaps against the rock, and I stare wide-eyed at it as he stomps up the stairs that are hanging off the side of the cliff.

The breath catches in my lungs, and I try not to recalculate our weight in my head. One forty plus two ten—my hands give a little press against his muscle tone once again, and once again I'm reminded that not a single part of him has ever tasted the bliss of a jelly doughnut—make that two twenty...

Just breathe. You're okay. Everything is okay.

"Fuck You Alice is turning a little white, Kais. Is that anything to be alarmed about?" Cat sways her hips with each gentle step up the stairs that she takes. Furry pink ears twitch against her hair as she studies my expression, and I blink repeatedly at the sight of them.

This is a dream. This is just a fucking dream nightmare.

The cracking of a board sounds out just before my body

jars against Kais's back. A screech rips through me, and my nails dig into his back.

He groans as he stiffens. His arms flex against the wooden railing on either side. Carefully, he snaps his fingers, and with ease we rise. The board cracks again, but this time it mends itself. Kais's spine straightens before he continues his task of carrying me higher and higher up the side of the cliff.

Cat waits, looking over the man's handy work before taking another gentle step. Her small shoulders shrug as she trails after us.

"So Fuck You Alice, where are you from, my darling?" Those ears shift again along her thick hair.

My eyes close, and a breath slips from my lips. I get to leave soon, right? When they decide I'm not Alice, I can leave. I might as well just tough it out until then. Get this over with.

"I just moved to California. I'm a freshman at the University of Southern California."

"Ah, the surface world. Such a terrible wasteland. I was a Princeton girl myself."

I blink up at the…cat woman…she's a cat woman.

"You went to Princeton?"

"Oh, yeah. I was one of their very first female graduates. Very scandalous. My mother cried about it for weeks."

I look up at her smooth skin. Her beautiful smile. Her perfect voluptuous figure.

"What year was that, Cat?"

Full lips pull into an alluring smile. "The nineteen seventies." It seems like a fond memory for her. It makes her happy, and it makes me confused.

She's young. Just a bit older than myself. But she's lived through the seventies…

"Where are you from, Kais?"

"Oh, you're asking me personal questions now. I don't think we're at that point in our relationship yet. I—literally—don't know your name, Prospect."

"Stop deflecting and answer her." Cat rolls her eyes with a sigh.

"My family came to America from Bordeaux, France."

There is a hint of an accent in his words. It's incredibly faint though. Hearing him speak of France is the first time I've actually heard the dip of his words. It's like saying the country out loud triggers the pretty accent in his tone. Aside from that, his English is perfect.

Thank God he didn't use the accent on me from the start or my infatuation with my captor would have blown right into planning the wedding of Mr. and Mrs. Fuck You.

"Tell her the other thing. Women love the other thing, Kais." Cat nods enthusiastically.

"Women do not love the other thing." He quiets for a moment, and I'm now genuinely curious about that other thing. Thankfully, he does tell. "I was a general in the Civil War."

"The winning side," Cat whispers while my head spins.

In my head, I swim through all the little middle school rhymes and tricks to remembering dates just to stutter out a vague timeline.

"In the eighteen hundreds?" My brow tenses as I blink hard at the ground.

"Yes."

"You're two hundred years old?"

"Not quite. Your math isn't nearly as good as I had hoped for a Prospect." His condescending tone is cutting and a little tired sounding, possibly from chasing after me and hauling me around this Kingdom.

A few more blinks at the ground don't help me understand their age at all. When I don't speak for several long seconds, he finally pities me enough to explain.

"In Wanderlust, time does not exist. It doesn't move forward. It doesn't progress. We're just here. Every day. Carrying on and waiting." His boots hit solid ground, and his steps become just slightly slower.

"Waiting for what?"

Bright light washes over the grass. Footsteps sound all around us, growing closer and closer until bodies press in on us.

"Alice. It's another Alice."

"This one's her, I just know it."

"It's her. It's her."

Voices carry and fingers snag against my dirty dress, but Kais just pulls me closer against his strong body.

When he speaks, his voice is low, barely a whisper among the chanting of that name.

"We're waiting for you, of course."

Chapter Five

We enter an estate of some kind, my fake blonde hair tangling around my face too much for me to see anything more than the floor. My ass hits shining tile, and once more, I'm glaring up into those careless sea blue eyes.

Warm golden light falls over us from big glass chandeliers overhead. They hang high on the domed ceiling, the towering walls making the room feel endless and extraordinary.

"It is my honor to present Fuck You." There's a noble sound to Kais's voice, and even he can't suppress the sarcastic glint in his gaze.

"I beg your pardon?" A woman's voice carries over the crowd of people who are staring down on me.

I turn on the floor, my muddy heels slipping against the tile, leaving a streak of filth in my wake. It takes effort to contain my modesty in the short—slightly destroyed—blue dress. My fingers smooth against the clumps of dirt clinging to the once soft fabric. I spent hours on this dress. Sewing and stitching and making it look perfect for my first college party.

And now the come stain on the hem is hardly noticeable. It's that bad.

My attention raises, and then I see her. Waves of silk bunch up to slim hips, a soft curve of her body, and delicate hands rest there. Long blonde hair curls slightly, and piercing gray eyes study every particle of dirt that I'm carrying around like armor.

Her chin tips up in a look of authority.

There are two golden thrones directly behind her on the far wall. All that's missing is a shining crown.

I've never met royalty before, but I know a queen when I see one.

"I said it's my greatest pleasure to introduce to you Fu—"

"My name is Madison Torrent." My voice rings out over Kais's adamant curse word.

Those steely eyes narrow on me. She crosses the wide golden tiles, coming closer and closer and closer. Until the ends of her sleek red gown kiss my fingertips.

"Stand up, girl."

It's been a few years since someone called me girl. The words *Sick Girl* spin through my mind, and my lips thin just thinking about it.

But I do as I'm told.

My heels click against the floor. Ashen particles of dirt drift down around me. It's like my very own confetti of filth. This woman doesn't seem to be too pleased about it.

"Profit. *Profit!*" Her voice snaps out the words.

My gaze drifts. Red hearts are painted on the golden doors we walked through. The same crimson hearts are embroidered into the hem of this woman's long perfect gown.

The Kingdom of Hearts…The Kingdom of Wanderlust. And a man who's obsessed with not being late.

I've dreamed up Wonderland. I'm in a sort of warped Wonderland.

I look to the loud and demanding woman before me. Is she the Queen of Hearts?

A young boy steps forward, parting the hundreds of people with ease as he drifts closer. The palest white hair I've ever seen lies in a disorderly state atop his head. Big brown eyes watch the woman closely as he takes his time striding over. It's an odd confidence to see in such a little boy.

When he's a foot away, I notice he only comes up to my shoulder. He's maybe five foot at the most. His shoulders and arms are slight and delicate. I can't help but wonder if he's even a teenager yet.

"Profit, the King has not yet come down. Can you please tell us if she is the one?"

The One. I'm getting very Harry Potter–Neo vibes here.

I mean, sure The One sounds prestigious and all, but those guys went through a lot of shit. A lot. And they had a whole team of friends to help.

What do I have?

I can't help but peer back at Kais. His attention never meets mine as he passes a lazy gaze over the crowd. He looks like he's ready to clock out the moment this woman says he's dismissed.

Yeah. I can't be The One. I don't have enough people who like me for me to be The One.

Warmth skims against my leg, soft and purring. A beautiful purple and pink cat sways between my heels, sending humming sounds of its contentment against my skin.

"She very well could be," the boy says.

No, I couldn't. Lack of friends, lack of good health, can't be The One. Sorry.

The boy's long fingers graze my hair, snagging on a tangled mess of the wig.

"She has the beautiful long blonde hair like I saw."

For a moment, I consider ripping off the wig, throwing it at his feet and telling him he can be The One, but that doesn't seem like proper royal etiquette.

"And the socks. Yes, she has the white socks."

These are the specifics we're tallying up for The One? The One is a blonde woman with white socks. Really? That's all it takes? The bar is set incredibly low for qualified applicants.

The woman looks down at the white, brown, and blood-stained socks. Well, they were white. Before I came here, they were definitely white.

"Is she here?" The low rumble of his voice is calm and curious. It calls my attention immediately.

The lighting of the chandeliers reflects off of the golden floors and highlights his skin to a godly tone. Blonde curls are neat and trimmed along the edges of the crimson crown that rests on his head. Dark gray eyes meet mine.

For a moment, the room is quiet. Not one whisper sounds through the room as his gaze holds on mine. My shoulders square for some odd reason as I look up at the man who must be the King.

"She says her name is Madison Torrent," the woman tells him.

"Madison." The deep tone of his voice hums against my name. He searches my features, and I'm still not sure what I'm supposed to say to any of them.

Not that they ask me for my opinion.

"And she's The One?" His attention slips to the boy who

stands between him and the woman.

"She has the socks."

Oh, for fuck's sake.

"There's only one way to know for sure." The woman's voice holds a hint of amusement. It's a cruel sound that makes me take a small step back from her and whatever it is she has in mind to find out if I'm their one true Alice.

As I step back, Kais steps forward. His arm brushes mine, and he never once looks my way. His jaw tips up to the woman, exposing his throat to her. The woman raises her hand, her index finger extending to show the shine of her sharp red nails.

She touches his neck lightly in an almost affectionate way that makes my stomach twist even more for some reason. Her nail rakes over his skin with an elegant wave of her hand. Smoke fumes from her fingertip and his skin. The distinct smell of burning flesh singes the air. When Kais grimaces just slightly, I lunge forward.

My hand grips her small wrist, and I tear her strange magic away from him.

"Just what do you think you're doing?" A thin line of anger seals her lips as she stares wide-eyed down on me. She's tall. Taller than myself even in my heels. But she isn't nearly as intimidating as she thinks she is.

A gentle warmth skims against my wrist.

"It's alright, Madison." At the sound of my name, I look up at him. His piercing blue eyes hold an exposed kindness to them. The anger and annoyance that he's had since the moment we met isn't there. It's a vulnerable look that disappears the moment he realizes it's there and too many people are watching. The vacancy in his gaze falls back into place.

The woman's attention slips past my hand gripping hers to peer down at the way Kais's fingers are resting against my wrist. It's that minuscule bit of attention that has him pulling away.

"Let's get this over with," Kais says coldly. His chin tilts up once more, prepared for the pain she's about to give him all over again.

This is a strange world. A strange place filled with customs and rules that I clearly don't understand. It takes me longer than a second to release her. My fingers are stiff as I pry them away one by one. My legs feel the same way as I take a careful step back.

And watch as she finishes her handy work of burning his flesh in front of her court of adoring subjects.

My brow lowers, and that tightness constricts even more within my stomach. A soothing warmth sways against my legs, and the cat is right there, tangling itself around me, giving me a meager amount of comfort.

Moments pass. Kais's teeth clench together hard as her finger grazes the strong angle of his throat and jaw. His lashes lower slowly, his breaths coming out in steady but deep exhales. And I wait with forced patience for the moment to end.

"There. Perfect. My best one yet, I think." Her pale eyebrows rise, a pleased smile widening her lips. "What do you think, Constantine?" She settles her assaulting hands back on her hips and takes a small step back for the King to admire her work.

"It's red, Sister."

"Red indeed, Brother."

Kais was just burned. Of course it's red. My jaw hurts from how much effort I'm putting in to keeping my mouth shut.

"That is an excellent sign, my King." The boy nods. The King nods. The King's sister nods. Every single fucking person in this room nods.

Except for Kais.

"What does red mean?" My gaze remains on the angry, fire

red numbers that are now etched across the side of Kais's throat. Thousands of black numbers and dates line his body. This one, 4884, isn't bleeding and scarred. It's smooth and perfectly healed. But it's crimson. Cherry red.

"Konstance possesses scribing magic. When she engraves dates or numbers into a person's skin, it'll bleed the truth about who we're looking for. She's a true asset to Wanderlust. Just like Kais. Kais has always been our man of judgement. A trusted advisor above all others." My lips purse harder when the King calls him their man of judgement. It's an infuriating title that just means he's their abused fucking prisoner of this world. He adds one more explanation that catches me off guard. "It has always turned black," he whispers.

"Always?" I can't help but repeat that word.

"It's never stayed red before."

A beat passes by with the thrumming of my heart.

"What does that mean?"

Kais turns, giving Konstance the span of his back as he faces me with a serious gaze that's hard to look at. It strikes nerves all through me.

"It means you're the One-est One we've ever received in Wanderlust."

"She's The One."

"The One-est One."

"She came for us."

"The One has come for us."

Shouting and chanting fire up from all around the open room. And I stand, staring up into those empty blue eyes.

"The One-est One. So I'm not The One, but I'm the best you've gotten?" I blink. I blink again. I try to make sense of all of the nonsense these people live in.

Alice is the final newcomer. This red number indicates I'm their Alice. I'm going to bring peace between two Kingdoms... I don't even know what the hell is wrong with the two Kingdoms aside from the moth lady and the centipede man. All I know is they have some kind of bug problem, and I don't have a clue how to fix that.

I am not equipped for pest control, folks.

"At the moment, yes, you're the One-est One." Kais's features are this smooth, careless but considering appearance. It's like his mind is turning, but there's so much he won't say.

He's a censored man in this Kingdom. My gaze flickers over the crowd.

Maybe they all are.

"What happens now?" Something bad. Something bad always happened to Harry Potter. Even when it was something good, it was always followed by something bad.

"If the red stays, you're her." Constantine keeps his perfect posture, but his attention is completely kind. He isn't a dangerous or cruel King. My gaze slips to his sister for only a moment. "We'll wait."

They'll wait. They've been waiting for hundreds of years. What's another few decades, right?

Shit, what if this takes decades? What if they insist I stay here, and it's a constant waiting game of wondering if that number against Kais's neck will ever fade to black?

I'm sick. I need medical attention too frequently to linger here. But the way they're looking at me, I know I can't leave.

It's no longer an option.

This isn't a land of Wonder like I've read in a thousand books before. This is a prison.

"I-I'm rather tired." The amount of effort I put into being

polite and proper is ridiculous. "It's been a tiresome journey."

"It certainly looks like it," the Profit says as he gives a once over of the blood and mud caked to my skin. I cut a hard glare toward the boy, but it goes unnoticed.

"Of course." Gentle gray eyes meet mine. Is he the King of Hearts? Knave? The White Knight? What role does he play if his sister is the Queen of Hearts?

King Constantine brushes his palm against the back of my hand, and it's a testing touch. An almost intimate touch, but I feel it. I feel the draw of his skin against mine. It's an unsettling tingling thing that coils energy all through my body.

Fuck, what if I *am* The One?

Chapter Six

King Constantine's sister dismisses us in a rush. I stand there watching her usher her brother through a door on the far side of the room. At the last second, she pulls the blond-haired boy along with her. He staggers behind them. She speaks in a rapid spew of quiet whispers. Constantine looks back at me once, his silver eyes searching for mine—just long enough for her to shove him along and slam the door shut behind him.

What a royal romance he and I are off to.

This is the shit fairy tales are made of, I'm sure of it.

Steady footsteps and booming voices sound through the room. Men close in from all corners of the room. Stiff black uniforms line their bodies. Only a single red heart on the left side of their coats interrupts the stark black jacket. I take a step back at the sight of them until my heels collide with sandy boots. The warmth of Kais's body bleeds into mine, but we never touch.

The guards guide the crowd out the massive double doors. The gold trim around the room, the cream-colored walls, and the

shining lights accent the touches of red that are scattered here and there.

The Kingdom of Hearts.

This is definitely a fairy tale world, except I can tell by the misery on everyone's faces that there are no happy endings here.

Not at all.

"Let's go. It's getting late." Kais's warmth slips away from me, leaving me cold and damp as he strides toward the dwindling crowd, taking his time to walk behind them.

I'm slow to follow after him. Everything about this place is bizarre. *Congratulations, you're The One we've been awaiting for hundreds of years.*

Now leave.

I'm only more confused than I was before.

It only makes sense to me because I think I feel the same way about them as they feel about me: they don't trust me. Alice is the legendary final newcomer. But she's a newcomer all the same.

"Konstance is probing him and the Profit for what their next move will be. I bet it's killing her self-control to wait." Cat appears out of nowhere and walks on gliding steps at my side. Her hair is a pale pink color, making her eyes appear even brighter in the warm lighting. It's all just small details that I couldn't see when we first met in the darkness.

My gaze is drawn to her clothes. The designer part of me thrums to life the moment I see the gorgeous gown. A tight silk dress hugs her chest, letting loose layers of the material act as sleeves against her smooth shoulders. An assortment of sheer black cloth and pale purple cascade down the back of her thighs, but only a triangle of fabric covers her front. It looks slightly like elaborate lingerie, but it makes her legs seem endless.

"Konstance isn't the Queen?" I ask in a quiet voice. Fewer

people are in the room now, the crowd being herded out by the dozens of guards.

Unladylike laughter shakes out of Cat, making her nose scrunch as her amusement grows louder.

Kais glances over his shoulder at the two of us with a stern look.

"Oh, she definitely wishes. No, she's just an advisor to the crown. The King's most trusted advisor, really. Even above Kais."

"Stop." Kais waits for us at the door, and though his tone is more of a growl than a whisper, we both pause.

"Stop what, pretty Rabbit?" Cat tilts her head slowly at him. It's a taunting look that only makes him glare back her.

He *is* the rabbit. The time obsessed rabbit. I knew it.

They're nearly the same height with her towering black heels. And Cat doesn't seem to be intimidated by the brooding man's attitude.

"Stop gossiping within castle walls. She'll have your furry head for your tone of voice alone, Catrice."

The cat woman flicks her long pink hair over her shoulder, her ears flitting with the movement, and sways past him, letting her heels click nicely against the tile as she goes.

"No one touches my hair. Even the King's sister knows that, Rabbit."

We watch her glide past the guards, raking her long pink nails down the front of their fine coats as she passes. She smiles sweetly when they squirm under her alluring attention.

She's beautiful. And a tease. Who was she before she came here? Was she the opposite of the sexy, confident woman testing the King's men?

I look up at Kais and consider the exact same thing.

We can be whoever we want to be here. That intrigues me in an unexplainable way.

I guess there's just more. I want more. I deserve to know more. And Kais is my guide. It's his job to tell me. He hasn't lied to me yet.

Still I stare up at him. His gaze drifts to me, searching my features for a moment while we stand in tense silence. There's a tension between us since the very moment he pulled me from the sea. Some of it is made of distrust, and some of it is made of conflicting admiration. I'm both skeptical and appreciative of the man standing at my side through all of this.

There's so much I want to ask him right now, but I can't find a single safe thing to ask him while we linger between the doors of the castle. His warning echoes through my mind. Right here, right now, is not the time to ask questions.

"Ready?" I ask in a small voice.

The look he gives me is almost regretful. It's a soft gaze that trails over my features like he's trying to figure me out as much as I'm trying to figure all of Wanderlust out.

His fingers press to the small of my back, and he lifts his other hand to gesture forward. And so we go.

The darkness washes over us, and he searches through the evergreen trees. My heels meet the wooden boards of the stairs that lead down the cliff. A hesitancy strikes through me, but I stiffen my shoulders and force myself to take the next unsound step. Since remission two years ago, I've made a lot of reckless decisions. I traveled the country with next to no money, I missed my mother's funeral because of traveling the country with next to no money, and now I'm here, trailing after a cat and my captor in a strange land.

I *have got* to work on my poor decision-making in the future.

43

A little part of me has grown careless of my mortality, especially since I've gotten diagnosed. *Again.* But there's just something about heights like this. It's too out of my control, I guess. I hate it.

A small whine comes from the board beneath my foot, but I pretend it didn't just threaten to collapse into a thousand tiny pieces into the terrifying waves far, far below.

I secretly consider attacking Kais once again just to see if he'll carry me down the rickety stairs. But I don't think that's the kind of thing Harry Potter would do, so it's probably best if I just continue on in a fearless way. My fingers dig into the railing with every step I take.

Completely fucking fearless.

"You're a slow thing, aren't you?" A black spike nearly stabs between my fingers as Cat slinks by, striding in her heels on the two inch hand railing as if it were a runway. The wind catches her long hair and the sheer ends of her beautiful dress, and her reckless image alone claws terror into my bones.

"Come along. Rabbit would never let you fall, darling." She turns the corner, so sure of herself and life that it leaves me stunned.

"She's right." His voice comes out as a rasp that fans against the back of my neck, forcing me to look back at him. A warm feeling passes through me from the sound of his sureness. I fully believe he'll never let anything happen to me. "The King would never forgive me if I let something happen to Alice. I'd be dead before you hit the ground."

I blink up at the carelessness of his words. The wind sweeps up my hair as I stare at him and the smirk that's teasing his lips.

"You're so sweet." I pull my attention slowly back to the stairs, and I start to make my careful way down them once again.

Several minutes pass and we're somewhere on the side of

the cliff when I realize it's probably safe to talk here. Kais and I are secluded on this trapeze of deadly stairs.

"Can I leave? When we reach the bottom, will you take me to the Dismay Forest?"

"No. It'd be impossible to get a newcomer into the other Kingdom even if I wanted to."

I stumble at the sound of his abrupt negativity. My foot slips through the stairs, and my heart falls right out of my chest, I swear it.

Warm hands wrap around my waist. His chest is hard against my back as he pulls me to a steady standing position.

"No?" I turn on him, my breathing still heavy from my near death experience, but this is more important. "You said I could leave if I wanted to."

"You're the One-est One." The seriousness he's able to hold in place while he says that ridiculous title makes me angrier. "You'd really turn your back on all the people who have been waiting on you for centuries? This Kingdom was made for Alice. And you're going to walk away."

"I don't *owe* them anything, Kais. I don't owe you anything." I've never owed anyone a single fucking thing, and this upside down fuckhole of a world is no different.

The moonlight makes his gaze lighter, more intense, washing out any hint of kindness within him.

"You don't owe me anything. You're right about that. But if you're a coward, maybe you *should* try to leave. You're not The One if you can turn away so easily."

A coward?

What are the people of the Kingdom of Hearts waiting for Alice to do? What am I getting myself into?

"What's the rest of the prophecy?" My arms fold as the

cold wind chills my skin with a shivering bite.

The way his eyes roam over me makes me wonder if he's sizing me up. In my three inch heels, he's maybe an inch taller than I am, and I don't know why my extra height gives me confidence. Is he trying to decide if I'm the strong, intelligent woman they've all been told about?

I'm not. I'm not the one they're waiting for. There are people out there with the ability to change the world. To inspire and to progress and to make a lasting impact.

That's not me. I don't have the optimism, and I don't have the health. It takes more than a nice wig and some white socks to make a strong person.

"There are rebels in Wanderlust. Those who are tired of waiting and tired of being neglected. Over a century has passed, and the Kingdom is happy to accept newcomers, but they're just as happy to forget about them too. They live in shambles. Fucking forgotten poverty." His jaw twitches, and his anger smooths before his voice can rise any more. "They're set on creating a new society with or without Alice in the neighboring Kingdom." He pauses as if it's hard for him to explain this. I guess he's never really had to before me.

"The Elders' Kingdom, Wonderland, they don't want us. They don't want newcomers. They don't like change." Cat walks by again, her arms out at both sides as if she's having fun balancing along the railing. "The land here isn't like the land in Wonderland. Nothing grows here. Nothing prospers. So the Rebel Hearts are willing to take Wonderland. No matter what the cost." Her heels click against the wood as she pounces by. There's a strange glint in the cat woman's gaze. It's a look of humor, but the words she speaks are anything but funny.

"And Alice will somehow cause amity between the Rebel Hearts and the two Kingdoms?" My attention shifts from Cat to

the cold look in Kais's eyes.

"Yes. That's what Profit believes. We can truly begin to live once she arrives. She will show the Elders of this realm that we're alike. We're just like them. We can all live here together. Alice will show them that." Kais's terse answers are harder to handle than Cat's twistedly happy ones.

"And she has to wed the King?" If I show up here tomorrow, will they throw a white gown on me and toss me into marital bliss?

That's fucking terrifying.

"No, you don't—*she* doesn't have to marry the King." Kais sighs a long and tired sound before bringing his attention back to me. "The King and his sister are the youngest Elders. This is their land, and the King thinks that by offering Alice a crown, it'll make her more likely to stay. It'll also show unity between the Elders and the newcomers. It'll ensure the safety of his people. He's offering her a once in a lifetime life in exchange for her aid."

Defeat pulls at my shoulders. The events of the day start to dig into me. It does sound kind of appealing in a way. Maybe it's the result of all those children's books drilling happily ever after into my youthful, naive mind. But it does cause an uncontainable spout of excitement within me to think I could be the Queen of…a fantasy realm. The Queen of Lust. Hmm, that sounds a bit like a porno. I'll have to keep working on my title, I think.

"Doesn't it seem odd that my name isn't Alice?" The rational part of my mind doesn't accept the fairy tale as easily as the absurd optimism that's trying to infect my thoughts.

"My name was Beatrice Smithson before I came to Wanderlust." I look over to find Catrice lying flat on her stomach, her feet tilted up and crossed at the ankle while she lounges lazily against the railing.

I try to pull my attention away from her carelessly dangerous position, but I can't.

"What was your name?" I finally look up at Kais.

He shrugs slightly. "My name was Kais St. Croix."

"And now it's Rabbit," Cat says with a smirk.

"That's an insulting name, and you know it. I transformed into a rabbit one time. What if I called you Cat Girl?" He tips his head up at his friend, and she ignores the look.

"Hmm, sounds kind of sexy." She rolls in one swift movement until she's lying on her back, looking up at the stars.

I'm here in the strangest of company. A woman who couldn't wait to form a new identity, and a man who couldn't even think of a new name.

I suppose I'd be more like Catrice, ready to give away my old life without looking back. But there's too much unknown here. With every new answered question, there are ten more unanswered.

"Are you two shape-shifters?"

"Yes," says Cat at the same time that Kais says no.

"*Okay...*" I exhale through my nose and consider just trying to find the Dismay Forest myself.

"I'm a shape-shifting shatter shrew." Cat lifts her hand and admires her flawless pink nails.

My lips part, but I can't decide if she actually just said words or not.

Kais shakes his head at her answer.

"It's not shape-shifting. Stop reading so many smutty books, Cat. We're illusionists. The Elders always called us illusionists. Our magic is different than theirs: more powerful, more pure because we're born from the sea." His jaw clenches slightly, pulling my attention to the shadowed ink of crimson numbers along his

neck.

Those are mine. Those numbers are mine. And they line his body like a lover's name.

I pull my attention back to Cat and force the thought away.

"Everyone here can do illusions like this? Change their appearance and stuff?" I glance from one of them to the other, but Kais is the one to answer.

"Takes time. Everyone here holds different levels of magic depending on how long they've been here." Kais looks bored out of his beautiful mind reciting this information to me.

It's all so different. Confusing. Alluring but confusing.

"If I leave, I'll just go back to my normal life?"

"Like I said, you're welcome to try to leave. The Elders may kill you the moment you pass the Kingdoms' divide, but you're welcome to just get out. I won't respect that decision, but you're welcome to do so. And if you stay, you'll gain all that Wanderlust has to offer. The magic of Wanderlust will infuse into your soul little by little, it'll change you. For the better." His tone is cold like he's already mentally cutting me out of his life.

Is that what he does? Keeps everyone at a distance, prepared to cut them out at any given moment?

It sounds exhausting.

The three of us stand there, hanging off the edge of a cliff while I stare starry-eyed up at my captor turned tour guide.

He all but just told me my life will be better here. For however long my life might have left. There's more in this land. I'm not the Sick Girl here, that girl whose mom died not long after she "beat cancer." I'm not that girl who's wasting her education on fashion design. I'm The Fucking One. *Kind of.* There's a life to be lived here. Any life I'd like, really.

If I accept it.

49

Chapter Seven

The hike through the forest is longer than I expected. Cat and Kais guide me through it, and for the most part, we travel in silence.

Until I spot them.

Mushrooms of red and gold glow along the floor. They cast light along the pine needles and give an alluring appeal to the simple little fungi.

"What are those?" I linger near a small group of them, letting them give my skin a crimson glow. They sway as I come nearer, as if they're aware of me as much as I am of them.

"Don't touch those." Kais snatches my hand in his and pulls me back until there are a few feet of space between myself and the tiny threatening mushrooms.

"Those are Marrigolds."

The word sounds familiar but holds a harsher tone than the pretty flower I'm used to seeing in the real world.

"Marrigolds are just hallucinogens. Rabbit is a little

touchy. I bet he'd finally relax if he had a small taste. You'd be so much more relaxed if you tasted things every now and then, Rabbit." Cat passes a taunting look to Kais, and in return, he passes her a quiet glare. "Healers prescribe them pretty frequently. Migraines, aches, pains, nausea. The usual."

"They use a hallucinogen for nausea?" My eyes narrow, but Cat only nods along, a big mischievous smile pulled across her lips.

"Wanderlust has an overly open policy about drugs. These things are the only thing that really takes to the soil here. They're like a miracle plant in the villagers' eyes." Kais releases my hand slowly and starts to walk on into the forest.

Cat nods once more before bending at the waist and breaking one of the sparkling mushrooms off. Its light pulses brighter for just an instant. She pops it into her mouth. The light of the fungus bleeds against her full lips as a smile slips into place there.

"Feeling a little light-headed from the trip down the mountain." Her smile is wide and glowing with golden colors when she looks at me.

"Yeah. Definitely. Take a hallucinogen to help with that dizziness." I nod a confused little nod but keep walking. I keep step with her as we follow after Kais. "Where are we headed exactly?" I ask.

A man drops down from somewhere up above. He lands in place between Cat and myself. "You're welcome to come home with me," the man whispers.

Oh. Okay. Bad pickup lines exist in every realm, it seems.

His hair is pulled back away from his face, leaving his deep dark eyes searching mine as a smile tilts his lips. The beard along his jaw instantly makes me realize how much of his face he's hiding beneath it. He's one of those guys who could be attractive with or without the facial hair, but he just doesn't seem to give enough of a fuck to shave.

"Has any female actually fallen for that line, Lighton?" Cat glances at the arrogant man at her side.

"Ah, not today, no. But the night is still young, pretty Kitty Cat." He walks with a swaying stature. His gaze darts around the forest as if there's more to be seen than what meets the eye. Where Kais holds stiff posture and brooding looks, Lighton is the opposite. Even the way he walks is elaborate and odd in a way.

He turns until he's walking backward in front of Cat and me.

"Lighton Farrow." He extends his hand, never once missing a step.

My hand slips into his. He squeezes, extending the feel of our hands held between us. He drags out the feel of my hand in his, his strength shown even in the simple handshake. Holy Fucking Wanderlust. This Kingdom is just made up of sexy, sexy—confusing—men, I swear.

"So, do tell. How quickly did the red fade out of your number?" His head tilts at me. "Cat here was the longest running One-est One, did you know that? Something like seventeen seconds for the red to vanish into black." His gaze drifts distractedly before coming back to me.

Cat smiles a pleased and alarmingly beaming smile.

"It's still red." The moment I say it, he stops walking backward. It's so abrupt that my heels hit against his boots, my palms pressing into his lean chest. My fingers slide slowly away from his warmth as I take a careful step back from the strange man.

"Still red? Like—still, still? At the moment? Currently? Presently? Right now?" He turns from me with a frantic spin before I can even speak. "Kais?"

He doesn't even ask before Kais's voice carries through the

dark.

"It's still red," Kais tells him from somewhere in the distance.

Lighton is slow to turn back around, his wide shoulders shadow over me, his amber eyes darting across my features at a rapid pace.

"It's still red." His voice is an empty sound as he looks at me once more. His attention trails over me a little slower as if it's the first time he's really seeing me. "Damn, you're a fucking train wreck, aren't you?"

A small tired smile pulls at my lips, and I can't help but nod. Aside from that little boy's sneering comment, Lighton's the first person to really be brutally honest about my appearance tonight.

It's refreshing. And insulting. I like it.

We follow after Kais. A tall and towering building streams up into the sky, surrounded by the glowing forest. It's an alarming but beautiful structure. It tilts unsteadily to one side and it only makes me more anxious when I realize that's where we're headed.

"Home sweet house," Lighton whispers.

"My home sweet house, you mean." Kais all but growls at the man at his side.

"Tomato, Toledo." Lighton shrugs good-naturedly.

My lips part at the weird word that most definitely is not the comparison I thought he was going for…

Kais narrows his eyes at the man as he turns the knob, but no one mentions Lighton's odd choice of words. It's like Cat and Kais are used to it while I'm left wondering what the hell it all means.

"When I open this door, there aren't going to be any unexpected guests?" Kais levels Lighton with a look.

"Does a shit bear in the woods?" Lighton asks with the most serious expression that doesn't reflect his completely fucked up words at all.

"*What?*" I glance from one person to the next, but Cat and Kais just shake their heads.

"A word of advice, don't drink the Rosen," Cat whispers strangely.

Everyone here is out of their minds.

"Just stop inviting rebels into my house," Kais grinds out as he pushes open the door.

"Of course. I wouldn't dream of it, my friend." Lighton has this innocent look in his big brown eyes, and I almost believe his sincerity.

Until a man comes crashing down in front of the door. An old golden chandelier clanks against the flooring right in front of Kais, and another dude comes ambushing the man who's clinging to the light fixture with both hands like it might still hold him up despite his new position lying at Kais's feet.

"Fucking hell, Lighton." Kais swings his glaring attention at the bewildered man by my side.

"What?" Lighton peers down at the men like he's just now noticed they're there. He lifts his innocent hands from his sides as another three strange men chase after the first two. "I don't think that's my fault." Lighton bites the inside of his cheek, and he looks genuinely confused about…everything…his entire life, possibly.

With a shake of his head, Kais strides inside.

Kais's house is a compilation of stairs. It's the most non-sensical home I've ever stepped foot into. The moment the door opens to the entryway, the four of us are greeted by steps winding up, up, up. The second floor leads off to a table with a chair and an old trunk for seating. We carry on past the lovely cracked dining

table. My feet ache when we come to the small third floor space. A tattered arm chair and twin bed with the covers thrown back takes up all the meager amount of space. A woman with tattered clothes dozes there, and I wonder if she too is an uninvited rebel. Judging by the glare Kais tosses her, I'd say yes, yes she is. We stride on past there as well.

From the first floor all the way to the top is an open stairwell, with the stairs leading to small platforms for each floor. It's odd and not at all a good use of structural space. It looks like this whole house might come tumbling down on a beautiful day with one slight breeze.

My heels falter against the top step that leads out to a large open attic space. Fabrics of all colors, silks, and hats string across the room like cobwebs long forgotten. Piles of the materials fill the corners of the room, and several people lounge there as well.

I like it. It reminds me of my classes back home. It reminds me of all the pretty racks of fabric I browse through when I want a new outfit. Except…messier.

The crowd in this room doesn't seem to mind the clutter. Laughter and echoing amusement carry over the sharp jarring music humming through the room. The people here aren't terrifying like the man I met on the coast. A woman passes by with antlers in her blonde hair and hooves clicking against the floor, but for the most part, everyone is fairly human in appearance. In the far corner of the room, standing atop a table, a woman plays a violin with deft fingers but off notes. She looks peaceful even as I grimace at the shrieking sound she's making with the little instrument. A man guides an unsteady woman across the dusty floor in an elegant but dramatic flair of dancing. It's a good effort, but really they couldn't keep in time with the harsh notes that are slicing through the room if they wanted to.

"Fuck, not again." Kais glares hard at the dozen or so people crowding his home.

The man dancing halts the moment he sees Cat and our little group. The man's height and the top hat on his head force him to duck beneath the strung-up fabrics. A smile of pure happiness clings to his handsome features when his attention lands on me.

"The Alice of the Moment, I presume." His warm palm pushes across mine, and with an elaborate bow, he presses his lips to my knuckles, just a gentle brush of his warm lips against my cold skin.

My eyebrow arches as he does the same with Cat, his lips lingering faintly against her skin before he glances heatedly up at the beautiful woman.

He's old school. He's Mr.-Darcy-leaving-a-calling-card old school, isn't he?

"Don't let him fool you, Brody was a performer on Broadway, not a Victorian gentleman," Lighton whispers with a carrying laugh.

The proper posture of the man in the three-piece suit drops as he pins a look to Lighton. "Why do you have to tell all of them that?" Brody's smile widens even more despite his performance being ruined. "It's still a pleasure to meet the Alice of the Moment."

"Want to tell me why there's a dozen Rebel Hearts in my house?" Kais takes a step closer to Brody. His perfect posture and the top hat tracing his dark hair make him impossibly taller than Kais.

"It's nothing. It's a non-party. The non-est-party I've never thrown." Brody's smile makes thin lines crease around his eyes. "They heard a True Alice had arrived. They wanted to celebrate with a non-party. Lighton and I were happy to oblige."

"Happy to oblige in my fucking house?" Kais is always so vacant, careful with his emotions; he's frightening when he's angry.

I wish I could understand it all though. Why are the rebels so rebelliously close to the King's castle? And why is Kais so familiar with them all?

Perhaps the Kingdom isn't as large as I thought it was. Maybe they knew each other before the rebellion started.

"Are you hungry? We've brought the most divine desserts." Brody's gaze trails from the mud clinging to my shoes to the tears in my dress to the wig pulling at my hair.

Before I can even reply, Kais is talking over me.

"Nothing *divine*. Not tonight, Brody." The two men stare at one another for a long moment. They couldn't be more different. Kais is all hard muscle and brooding looks while Brody is delicate with carefully veiled thoughts, a smile that doesn't reflect his intentions at all.

"Let me get you a drink. Some form of welcome must be made for the Alice of the Moment."

"*Do not* get her a drink." Kais takes a single step until the two men are nearly toe to toe. Shining shoe to muddy boot.

And I'm standing at the sidelines, all eyes on me: the woman they're speaking over because, clearly, I don't have a voice of my own.

Guess they didn't teach too many Victorian formalities on Broadway.

My nails dig into my palm, and the faint feel of Cat's fingertips brush down the side of my arm.

"What about a bath? You look like you're in desperate need of a bath, Love," Brody swings his attention back to me.

"No—"

"A bath would be fantastic. The Alice of the Moment would love a bath, thank you for asking." I glare intently into Kais's eyes as I step past him, placing my palm lightly in Brody's open hand.

His eyebrow cocks high as he passes Kais. I ignore the two men's taunting looks and just let Brody lead me toward a dark staircase on the far wall. Lighton trails after us on quiet swaying steps.

When my heels click against the first step, I realize how secluded I am with the two strangers. These beautiful strangers.

Would a rebel harm the beloved Alice? Would they hurt me? It just goes to show how little I know about Wanderlust politics and the place I stand in the middle of all of it.

It'd look pretty pathetic if I died trying to prove a petty point to Kais over a bath.

"It's sensible to trust your senses, Love." Brody's mellow timber is meant to calm me, I think, but his phrasing doesn't do anything of the sort.

"It took me years to ever really feel that I belonged here. It's understandable that you don't understand this. That you don't trust us. Or me." He peers back at me, his dark eyes meeting mine in the shadowy stairwell. He holds my gaze for several seconds before opening the door. The three of us are close, my arm brushing along his, but he holds me at a careful distance. A respectable distance.

Cold wind hits my face, tangling my hair in an instant. His fingers lace with mine as he leads me into the night air. The man faces away from the wind and lights some kind of cigarette that drifts too much white smoke around us. I look away from the strange cigarette and the oddly sweet smell it's wafting.

It takes me a second to realize we're on the roof of the towering building Kais calls his home. My heels scuff against the concrete as confusion settles in.

Lighton pushes the door closed with a heavy click. When I look back at him, he's leaning lazily against it, watching me

through his hooded brown eyes.

"Where's the bathroom, Brody?" I halt in my tracks, and he turns to me slowly.

"The bath house is just over there. The set-up of this house is set *right up*." Brody's points toward the sky and his play on words makes me pause after everything he says to try to find the simple meaning. He gestures with a wave of his hand to the large green-house-looking room off in the corner of the roof. It's just mere inches from toppling right off the thin building, really. Beams of… *are those books*? Two fragile looking columns of literal literature hold up the structure that teeters out off of the side of the house.

Talk about a cliff hanger.

Neither of the two men hesitates as they stride right through the glass door. Brody flicks the cigarette to the ground before swinging open the foggy door for me.

My heels click uneasily against the slate gray flooring. On the far wall, leaning out over the edge of the house, sits a large bath. It's one of those several person type baths which means it holds more water, more weight to come crashing down if those stacks of books give out beneath this room.

Perfect.

I swallow slowly before coming closer to the inviting hot water. The glass walls of the room are dotted with condensation, water trails down the sheets of glass, and twinkling lights blur from the city beyond.

It's…odd but beautiful.

Once again, a door clicks closed with an announcing sound and I glance back at watchful brown eyes. Lighton leans against the door there. If I didn't know Cat was a literal cat, I'd think Lighton was too just from the waiting look he's giving me right now. He looks every bit ready to pounce.

I pause there looking at the two men who watch me intently.

"Do you want me to go first?" Brody shrugs out of his sleek black coat, revealing the soft material of his black button up.

My heels take a clicking step back.

"No." I lift my hands, unsure what to do now that I've gotten myself into this fantasy of a situation. I can't think of a better dream than having two sexy men slide into a bath with me. In reality, all of this is a bit fucking much. Deep down, I want to be carefree and sexy, but it's hard to be that person when I have no real experience. It was easy to pull Austin, Texas, behind a tree and prepare for utter disappointment. I was drunk and had plotted the moment all week.

I'm painfully sober right now in front of these beautiful men.

"Can you just—turn around?"

Lighton passes Brody a look, and the shared moment makes them smile. The cat that got the canary is definitely in their features right now.

Slowly they both turn on their heels. Brody leans a shoulder against the glass wall while Lighton waits with his hands carefully tucked into his pockets.

The toe of one shoe presses against the back of the other, and I kick the heels off quickly. I don't know why it feels like a race to undress before they turn around, but it does. My fingers shove off the socks caked in dry mud, and the moment I slip out of the destroyed dress, I feel lighter. And naked. Literally.

I dip into the hot bath as fast as my pounding heart will allow. It stings against my skin, but I submerge myself deeper, not even pausing to untangle the clips of the wig from my hair. It's easier to just leave the messy wig on and relax for now. It feels amazingly soothing. I don't look down at the steaming water though.

My gaze holds on them as they turn slowly around. Brody doesn't undress, but he comes closer, touching his fingers lightly to the surface of the water. Pink light ripples out from his touch, and flower petals drift up around his palm, drifting out on the rings of shimmering pink until they're spread all around me. The small rose petals skim against my skin, filling my nose with a beautiful scent that's too strong to really be rose.

When I look up, Lighton's eyes darken to an almost black color as he looks at me from across the small room. His hands fist in the collar of his black shirt, and he pulls it away within seconds. Hard lines veer down his stomach in delicious squares.

Shit.

I've never seen a man as muscular as Lighton naked.

And I'm about to now. I inhale deeply on a shaking breath, and the floral scent fills my lungs, making me cough just lightly.

His fingers shove down his black skinny jeans, taking his boxers with them in an instant.

"I guess you don't want me to turn around," I whisper more to myself than anyone.

"Mmm and miss the look on your face? Never." His teeth sink into his lower lip as he strides toward me.

You know when someone points to an enemy, and you try real discreetly not to look but fail miserably? Lighton's cock is the enemy right now.

I fail. Miserably.

My lashes flutter as I look to his face, down, look to his gorgeous face, look down, finally catch sight of—fuck. I swallow the moment I see it.

Fun fact that I haven't admitted to anyone here: I'm a virgin.

Between being labeled the Sick Girl and losing my mom

earlier this year, I've never had a normal sexual experience.

A rush of restless energy soars through my veins all at once, giving me a heady feeling as I breathe in the warm bath water. In this moment of knowing my cancer returned just last month, I want that experience.

And Lighton looks like the guy who wants to give it to me.

Even if I weren't inexperienced—I mean, there was that time sophomore year of high school that Jared Porter fingered me for a grand total of four minutes in his car before dropping me off from our date, but that hardly counts—but even if I weren't inexperienced, I'd think that Lighton's is impressive. It arches up toward his lean stomach, and he smiles when I finally meet his eyes again.

"Like what you see?" He licks his lips slowly.

I close my mouth with a snap and wet my lips before pushing a look of indifference into my features. "I've seen better."

I. Have. Not.

That casual smirk is still in place when he lifts his leg over the edge of the tub and sinks down at my side. An odd silver chain bracelet is all he wears, his arms spread out along the edge of the tub as he relaxes, his fingers nearly touching my shoulder. My lashes close slowly as I take a deep breath of the warm, intoxicating water. My fingers glide distractedly through the hundreds of red, glittering petals as another wave of strange, slow emotions swirl through me. It's the most alluring but confusing sensation.

It's a drunken energy that's soothing and tiring all at the same time.

Brody comes closer, rolling his sleeves up to his elbows. Tattoos line his left arm. A weird rabbit that reminds me of a nineties band is on his forearm with the green mushroom from Mario just beneath it and then other brightly colored whimsical animals

and symbols drift up from his wrist and sneak beneath the line of his shirt sleeve. If I didn't know he wasn't a Jane Austen gentleman, I do now.

He sits at the edge of the bath, never undressing, only letting his fingers slice through the water, creating more and more pink blooming ripples with every move of his hand. When I look up at him, he's inhaling another cigarette to his lips again. A perfect ring is blown out on a steady exhale. He sends ripples through the shimmering red petals, and another strong waft of that alluring scent fills my lungs. The smoke, the water, it's all an addicting taste that I know I shouldn't submerge myself into the way that I am.

My eyes close slowly once more. Brody led me here. He's fully clothed and keeping a nice distance between us… I wonder if the look he passed Cat meant anything. I can't really picture the two of them together. She's too eccentric, and he's too proper.

On and on my mind drifts about to most mundane things.

I wonder if Kais will join us for a bath soon… Everyone has to bathe sometime, right? Why am I so obsessed about his cleanliness all of a sudden?

Because I want him dirty…

Yeah. That's definitely the real reason.

"You're not the One-est One they're looking for, are you, Madison?" Brody's tone is calming as he takes another puff, his fingers trailing through the water between Lighton and the wall.

I blink up at him, and my mind feels tired now. Sleepy.

A smile pulls at my lips as I consider that title. One-est. One-east, Onest. Wontst. A giggle tumbles from my lips, and Lighton laughs maniacally with me, his slick fingers skimming down the side of my shoulder. At the small contact of his skin against mine, I come closer to him, my body drifting through the water that's feeling a bit too thick now.

My body thrums when my legs meet his, and he wastes no time pulling me onto his lap. Tingles like I've never felt wash over me as cool air meets my breasts. Water trickles down my skin when I lift slightly to straddle myself over Lighton's lean hips. He smiles that alluring smile of his, but his hands hold in place against my hips.

What I wouldn't do to feel his hands all over. To let his fingertips explore every part of my body in the slowest possible way.

And then my core settles against the thickness of his cock.

Fuck his fingers. Fingers are overrated. This, this is what I never knew I needed. I shift over his length, letting the underside of his cock brush against my clit just right. We both exhale an unsteady breath, inhaling more of that sweet scent of the water.

"Is it big? It's big isn't it? What's the average for men, eight, nine inches?" I whisper my question to him, my eyes widening as if it's hard to keep focused on his gentle amber eyes.

Lighton and Brody both laugh at my words, but I don't know why.

"Mmm, you're just innocent enough to make me think you *are* Alice," Lighton says in a quiet voice tinged with sadness. "I know Kais hopes you are. I hope you're not."

"Why?" I breathe out that word as his palms start to wash away the dirt against my skin. Long fingers glide along my throat, his thumb skimming against my jaw in such a delicate way it causes the air in my lungs to catch.

My thundering heart becomes louder when his fingers dip down, barely skimming the curve of my breast before coming back up to my collarbone.

My heartbeat is still fluttering even as he says the strangest thing. Stranger than usual, I mean.

"Because if you're Alice, you'll hate me soon enough."

Chapter Eight

I'm still staring down at the beautiful man with his confusing words and charming smile. He always says the most confusing things with the sweetest smile on his lips. I can't make sense of it.

Nothing here makes sense. My head is pounding, and I can't seem to think straight to save my life.

"You're the hare, aren't you?" My voice sounds far off, my mouth hovering just above his.

He'd be a good kisser, I bet.

"I'm a man. *Sometimes*. Sometimes I'm a man."

His fingers catch in my wig, pulling at it until his brow creases.

"And sometimes?" My fingers push along the dark stubble of his jaw. The lighting flecks golden colors among the dark. Golden just like his long hair that's tied back from his face. He has a man bun. I wonder if man buns were popular during the time he was on…what did Cat call it? The surface. I wonder if they were popular when he was on the surface or if he's just naturally sexy like this.

"Sometimes I'm a man. Sometimes a rabbit. Sometimes I'm nothing more than smoke in the wind. Depends on what the occasion calls for. Job for the dress you want, not for the dress you have and all that."

I arch an eyebrow at him, but a smile pulls at my lips.

Kais is the white rabbit obsessed with time, and Lighton is…that other manic one that drinks too much tea. The March Hare.

"So you are the hare?"

"I don't know what you mean," he whispers.

We're smiling at one another, running our fingers all over each other's bodies slowly until we're just breathing each other in with the warm delicious floral scent of the water. His fingers hesitate when they slide over my collarbone. He holds my gaze as his fingertips trail lower and lower and lower, tracing down along the water droplets against my skin. The water and the feel of his light touch is enough to make me shiver.

His palm just grazes over my breast when the door opens, drifting cold wind over my heated skin instantly.

"What the fuck are you doing?" Kais's glaring gaze shifts from Brody who's watching me in his friend's arms to Lighton who still hasn't taken his eyes off of me to notice the angry man storming into the room.

"We're questioning the enemy for you, of course," Lighton says with that sensual smile pulling at his lips. White teeth give a full perfect smile among his scruffy beard, and my heart flutters at the sight of his happiness.

"Yes, this looks like a very standard interrogation." Kais's jaw tightens, and his stormy eyes only lose track of that anger for

a second when his gaze dips low to follow the movement of Lighton's fingertips sweeping so slowly across my nipple.

When my breath catches, Lighton smirks, his gaze held fully on me, focused for possibly the first time since I met him.

Lighton's hands rise, and he wipes away something on my cheeks before pushing his fingers…under my wig instead of through my hair. Another crease of his brow as his hands stay locked in place between the clips and the mesh.

Oh. That's awkward.

"She's Alice, okay? Stop trying to fuck her before the King's sister cuts your cock off. The numbers are red. She's Alice." Kais's voice grows louder, interrupting the haze in my mind as I look up at the scowling man. "Her socks were white, her hair is blonde, you can see she's Alice."

And that's the last straw.

With a huff, my fingers tangle into the matted blonde locks. My scalp stings as the clips pull against my hair. I actually really liked that wig. Strands of my hair had started to fall out just this week from the chemo. The wig was thick and beautiful where my hair was thinning.

I swallow down my self-consciousness at revealing my red hair that's plastered against my head. It used to be so damn shiny. Long and beautiful. It's still long, but it hasn't been pretty since I was a little girl.

I toss that stupid wig and the little black headband at Kais's feet. Before he can yell about it anymore, I dip my head under water. I slip away from Lighton and his fantastic cock and push my hands through my hair over and over and over again. I push at it until the sweat and the dirtiness is gone, and all that's left is the sinking feeling that I'll never be a normal woman. I'll never be that pretty girl that gets to make fun mistakes with a guy like Lighton.

A part of me will always be that bitter Sick Girl.

When my face surfaces and I breathe in the steamy warm air, I'm met with the rage of Kais's gaze.

"Are you fucking crazy? Put this shit back on before you get us all killed."

I never thought he could be more on edge than he already was.

Until now.

Kais

I swear this woman's going to fuck up a Kingdom as well as a rebellion.

History is full of beautiful women making stupid men do stupid fucking things to the point of destruction. That's what I see when I look at this beautiful fucking woman: destruction.

It's in all of us, really. I've seen the darkest parts of the world. War might be riddled with death, but there are far worse things than dying.

I see dark things when I look at this innocent girl with the big green eyes.

And right now, I need her to play this part for all it's worth.

"Put the fucking animal pelt back on."

"Animal pelt?" Her upper lip curls. She does that a lot when she speaks to me. She looks at Lighton with interest and curiosity. She looks at me like I do nothing but confuse and disgust her all at the same damn time. "It's a wig. Human hair."

"That only makes it worse, Prospect."

Lighton and Brody both nod in unsubtle agreement.

I consider my little pet name for her. I can't bring myself to call her by her name when I know she'll change it. They always do. Everyone's so quick to change themselves here.

I also can't bring myself to call her Alice though either. It's a lie and I know it. I knew it the moment I met her and she was out of her mind babbling about fucking orgasms of all things.

It's easier if I just pretend she's a nameless newcomer to me. I'll call this confusing woman Prospect until the day she marries the King.

And she will marry the King.

Light shines off of her deep red locks, and I notice how far she's sunken down into the intoxicating Rosen Bath since I entered the room. I hate how much I keep thinking about her breasts pushed up against Lighton's chest.

Were they fucking?

I shake my head at the drifting thought that I can't seem to push aside.

Brody is a cocksucker for giving her a drug she doesn't even realize is absorbing slowly through her skin with each minute that ticks by.

"Get out of the Rosen. Put the hair back on and *do not* take the fucking thing off again." My voice is more growling than I intended, but she doesn't even blink at the sound of it.

I need to calm down. I need us to be friends of sorts. But she's such a fucking mess she makes it impossible for me to breathe easy without wondering what she's diving face first into next.

Like Lighton's cock.

"I'm actually enjoying myself. Maybe I'll stay here for a while. Maybe I'll never leave the Rosen. Maybe as the future Queen of Lust"—she winces at that strange title but carries on—"maybe I'll demand my loyal subjects to…entertain me right here." She sends a sultry smile at Lighton, and when he smirks back at her, anger strikes right through me. He shifts, pushing off from his spot near the edge to glide toward her.

My hand grips his slick shoulder, sloshing him right back in place in an instant.

"Get. Out. Of. The. Fucking. Bath. Madison." My jaw clenches. Her eyebrow arches.

Everything with her is a fight. Nothing is easy.

I hoped she'd be resilient not impossible.

"Don't be an asshole, Rabbit." Lighton turns his ridiculous amusement on me, and when he smiles, it takes everything in me not to knock my fist into his messy mind. "Join us. But—enter at your own risk, she thinks nine inches is very average."

Did I say she was impossible? I meant unbearable.

Brody and Lighton exchange a quiet laugh, and I'm still glaring down at the two of them. If she lingers for another twenty minutes in the Rosen, she'll be as crazy as Lighton.

That's it. I'm done. Play time is over.

I shove past Lighton, over Brody's trailing fingertips. Warm water saturates my pants as I stomp into it. It sloshes over the edges in heaps. A creaking sound comes from the flooring, but I ignore it. My fingertips meet her slick curves, and for the second time tonight, I toss her over my shoulder. This time, it's harder to find a platonic place to grip ahold of her. My palms slide against her thighs, and I'm all too aware of how close my hand is to her hot pussy. My boots skate against the bath as her screech echoes through the room.

"I knew you'd want her for yourself. You can't be a hero with an erection, Kais." Lighton's fucking words trail after me as I carry her to the door, suddenly aware of just how hard my dick actually is.

When Lighton Farrow makes an accurate statement, it's startling. Why can't he be right about something else? *Anything* else.

Before I rush away from him, I grab a white towel and toss it over the distracting curve of her ass as I head out into the night air.

"Put me down."

The moment she says it, I drop her to the ground.

"What the fuck?" She wraps the towel across her, draping it over her nudity and her perfect tits. Of course she has perfect tits. Not blonde hair and perfect tits. It's a cruel distraction. That's just not what we need from the One-est One. Her numbers turned red for fuck's sake.

The King isn't going to waste time. He'll want her to be Alice.

Even if it's glaringly obvious to anyone who speaks to her that she isn't.

I kneel down, meeting her narrowed green eyes. I've waited almost two hundred years in a crumbling Kingdom for an Alice to show up. I have a choice to make: Tell the King that she's not Alice.

Or…

Use her for a better cause.

She's not going to like that. Know what women don't like? Being used. It's a hard suggestion to wrap your head around for anyone, really. There was a time when it was all I knew though. I was a tool for the military. I was being used in a way. I was some-

thing to be used for a greater good.

And now I'm being used once again.

For a rebellion.

If the Elders' Kingdom, Wonderland, doesn't accept us, we'll take it. No one should live like this. But with Alice, there's a better way. A peaceful way.

We just need an Alice.

"What do you have in your life up on the surface?" I study the emotions that sneak across her face. She's good at hiding them. Now that the Rosen is in her system, she isn't nearly as careful with them as she thinks.

A flash of angry sadness pulls at her mouth. My tongue glides across my lips the moment my gaze catches against her pouty mouth. I don't know what causes that look. Nothing good.

Which, to be honest, is good. *For us.* Not for her.

"I'm getting a degree. I want to be a designer."

"Clothes? You want to make clothes?" The harsh tone of my voice makes those pretty eyes glare hard at me. It should be strange how much I like the hateful way she looks at me. It's the only time I see her real emotions though. I see a fight in her, and that's strong and sexy. I like seeing that fight.

I lead a lot of people from the surface into Wanderlust. Of all the people I've brought, none of them have been as confusingly frustrating as Madison.

"Yes, I want to make clothes."

"What about your family? Any kids? Husband?" My words are sharp and to the point and piss her sexy lips off even more.

Good.

"No," she answers quietly. "It's just me." A small pause

slips in, and then she shows me more of herself than she has the entire time she's been here. "My mom died a few months ago. It's just me."

Those three sad words at the end repeat and repeat and repeat in my mind. It's sick how happy they make me. There's nothing better to fuel a rebellion like total fucking loneliness.

That's really good for us.

Madison

The clothes he gave me are old. A thin cotton shirt and tattered pants make me wince to even look at them. With an angry yell and more than one or two curse words, he ran off the rebellious partygoers. And now we're alone.

The memory of me straddling Lighton's cock is seared into my mind, and I cannot believe I did that. What was wrong with me?

And why, within a matter of twenty-four hours, have I been pressed against two men's cocks and *not* had sex? Is it broken? Is my vagina broken? Soon she'll spend her days sitting on an old dusty shelf, remembering her sad glory days of all the men who tried to grind her gears and failed. When all along all she was missing was one good screw.

I sigh a pitiful sound at the memoir I'm painting of the *Little Vagina that Couldn't*.

My throat clears when I look up at the serious man staring

down on me.

I shift under his disappointed gaze.

His bedroom feels smaller with me sitting at the edge of the mattress and him lingering near the stairs. A blanket of mismatched colors is tucked in tightly to the small mattress, and all I can think about is how I haven't made my bed a single time this year.

What is the point? Really? It seems like the most monotonous task. What a waste of four minutes. And trust me, coming from a girl who's suffered at the hands of Jared Porter, I know a wasted four minutes when I see it.

My gaze catches my reflection in the warped mirror on the wall near the end of the bed. The dim lighting shines against it, and the woman who stares back at me startles me. My breath catches as my reflection shows my big green eyes. My hands push through my thick red hair. I move a little closer to it and look for the dark circles under my eyes.

But they're not there.

My skin tone is flawless. My throat constricts, and I push once more to the back of my head, searching out the small bald patch I'd found just this morning.

But it's gone.

Only glossy hair meets my fingertips. My hair hasn't been this thick and beautiful in years. Silky strands fist through my fingertips over and over again as I stare in wonder.

"What?" I whisper the word, but I can't bring myself to say anything else.

"What's wrong?"

I blink at my reflection even as I feel his gaze against my skin.

Am I...cured? I try to think through the stories of Won-

derland that I remember, but I don't ever recall Wonderland healing anyone.

I don't remember a Kingdom called Wanderlust there either, so maybe I can't rely too heavily on the storybook.

At the same time, I can't help but let the hope in my chest bloom. I can feel it. I felt stronger the moment I landed in a heap on the sandy shore of that Island.

I shake the thoughts from my head. I don't want him to know I'm sick. *Was?* Was sick? Maybe it's stupid, but I don't want my old life to carry into this place. If I truly am healed, I don't ever want to be that Sick Girl again.

I swallow down the thick feelings rising in my chest.

His attention is still searing across my skin.

"Why do you keep looking at me like that?" I don't look up at him as I push my fingers through the few holes lining the hem of my white shirt.

I'm making new clothes first thing tomorrow morning. Maybe I'll make a few extras for the rebels who were here tonight. I could hand them out like non-party favors at the next one of Brody and Lighton's non-parties.

"I'm going to ask you something, and I want you to consider it. And then never ever speak of it again." His arms fold across his broad chest, making the inky lines around his biceps bulge with the intimidating stance.

I fold my arms as well but don't reply.

"*Never*," he repeats sternly as he tilts his head down to meet my gaze.

What is with this guy? Can he do anything without being Captain WonderPrick? Why is my hero such an ass?

"*Okay.*" I stretch the word out for him until he nods happily.

"I want you to pretend to be Alice."

"So you agree that I'm not."

He nods slowly, never taking his eyes off of me.

"I think you want to stay here. And I think you and I can help one another." His rumbling voice is quiet and rasping. Alluring when he isn't angry. Beautiful even.

"What do you want from me, Kais?" When I lift my gaze to meet his, he trails over my features carefully. I see him. I see him studying every little thing, even if he thinks he's being discreet.

My eyes roll when he continues to watch me.

"I want you to be Alice."

"And what about when the real Alice shows up?"

"Could take decades. I need you now."

I need you.

I shift against the little bed until it squeaks at my constant movements.

"If they accept you as Alice, they'll try to mend the peace between the two Kingdoms. Alice is the final puzzle piece. An Elder made all of this possible. Someone wanted Alice to be here. King Constantine won't contact the Elders' Kingdom until she's arrived. He wants her. He's obsessed with the thought of her."

"You want me to marry some dude who's obsessed with me. Sounds creepy. And dangerous."

"I want you to set the ball into motion. He needs to take care of this city, or they will rebel and it won't be good for anyone. You have the ability to stop a war. The people here need you. They need an Alice."

My throat tightens. It's weird, but he didn't really have to argue too hard. This place is healing me. I can feel it. I'd stay no matter what he asks me to do.

My gaze collides with the most hopeful blue eyes. They're filled with pleading emotions, and my heart sinks every time Kais shows me something real.

"Then, I guess I'm your Alice, Kais."

The smallest of smiles pulls at one side of his full lips. He settles into the arm chair near the bed, our knees meeting, almost touching as he leans back in the seat. "Get some sleep then. We leave to meet with King Constantine in exactly four hours. We can't be late."

His head tips back against the gray chair. It's cushioned, patched with black cloth in a few places with a high headrest, intricate wooden armrests that shine in the dim lighting. It's nice, but it's parlor furniture, really. It doesn't look at all comfortable.

"Is that where you're sleeping?" I shift uneasily on the small bed that I know is his.

"Well this Un-Alice dropped in a few hours ago, and as you and I both know, Alice is destined to be the Queen of Lust. Can't have a Lusty Queen sleeping on the floor."

My eyes close, and he's terrible at teasing, but I do know teasing when I hear it.

Why did I call myself the Porno Queen of Lust out loud?

But I am a Queen.

"Queen Madison Torrent. I like it." I shimmy up the bed and slip beneath the blanket as I watch him shake his head slowly at me.

"Queen Madison Torrent will never live in this world, Prospect." His voice is low and regretful. It tingles across my skin until I shiver as my stomach twists tightly from the sound of his words. "You're the future Queen of Wanderlust. A false queen but a queen all the same. Queen Alice Liddell."

A soft pillow caresses my new healthy hair, and I think

about his words for over an hour. I dwell on what I'll have to do tomorrow for so long the morning sunlight starts to peek in through the white curtains. Tomorrow I'll start my path as a traitor to the throne. If anyone finds out what Kais and I are plotting, I'll be hung, cut into quarters, beheaded. Whatever it is royals like to do to traitors like me. Even with all that hanging in the balance, all I can think of is one thing:

I'm Madison Torrent, False Queen of Wanderlust.

Chapter Eleven

Madison

The matted and muddy hair is tossed in my face first thing in the morning. It's a very charming wake up call to say the least. My fingers fist into the coarse, dry strands of the wig, and I shove it away like it might infect my beautiful new hair just by touching it.

"You'll need to comb through it a bit before we leave this morning." Kais stands expectantly over me, his handsome but stern face is the first thing I see.

Until I roll over and pull the pillow over my head to block out the golden morning sunlight.

"Nope," he says. The pillow is ripped away, and I can either shield my eyes with the destroyed wig or be an adult and roll my ass out of the warmth of this bed.

Option three: I pull the blanket up and snuggle down into it like a hamster burrowing into a nest.

It too is ripped away. The air is colder now, chilling against my skin as I curl into myself.

"What time is it?" I mumble, curling up tighter as if sleep is still a silver lining possibility.

"It's three minutes after we were supposed to leave. Get up."

"Mmm, let her sleep. She's sexy all curled up." The bed dips at the sound of his smooth voice. A voice like sex itself. Lighton's low rumbling tone hums through me, bringing my body to life. And that, that is what wakes me up.

I turn until I'm flat on my back again. Honey-colored eyes stare down on me through a hooded gaze. The memory of me wrapped in his arms last night, our bodies slick and hot against one another, flashes through my mind. A blush creeps up my cheeks before I can swallow the memory back down.

"Good morning, sunshine." That rasping tone of his voice and the low lidded appearance of his gaze are sexy, but I can't help but wonder how much he's drunk this morning. A manic smile pulls against his lips, revealing perfect white teeth. The smile only adds to my original thought.

A part of me aches to know why he's trashed at six in the morning. What dark shadow is cast over his life to make him so adamant at blocking it out first thing? Lighton is beautiful, the appearance of perfection, but there's something beneath the surface he isn't showing. Something he seems to want to forget.

And I want to know what it is.

I push slowly up until my back hits the headboard.

"I said we're late," Kais growls the words out. "Throw the human mane on and let's go." He folds his arms with heavy impatience.

"I can't wear this wig, it's destroyed." My fingers trace over the tangled locks, the torn netting and the broken clip in the back.

I look up in time to see the tic in Kais's jaw as he appears to bite back whatever words are lashing through his mind.

"Have patience, Rabbit. Don't you know that things are good to those who cum?" Lighton specifically says that last word with a wiggle of his eyebrows, and it only makes Kais glare harder at his friend.

"You mean good things *come* to those who *wait*." Kais's lips barely move as he speaks through clenched teeth.

"No. I think you're wrong with that one." Lighton turns to face me once again, ignoring the way Kais shakes his head in annoyance. He reaches for me, his manic eyes sweeping over my features. Long fingers push back my hair. It's the gentlest touch that locks up my muscles from his closeness. I relax the moment his fingers thread through one side of my hair. My chin tips up, and he holds my gaze as he comes closer. He kneels, towering over me as he touches me so softly.

And then roughly.

His fist tightens in my silky locks just as his Adam's apple bobs, his gaze sparking with a look that's a mixture of lust and lucid concentration. His head lowers and his hand pulls down, arching my neck until I meet his stare. A second passes as his lips ghost over mine, his gaze searching back and forth.

"Perfect pain. Perfect pleasure," he whispers hypnotically against my lips.

My breath catches from the feel of his strange words against my tongue. A smile tips the corner of his mouth. And then he pulls away. I'm left blinking up at the alluring man and his constantly odd behavior.

"Was that really necessary?" Kais passes a new glare toward the man kneeling at my side.

"Well, I got the job done. All you did was growl about it." Lighton's smug amusement doesn't falter, and the moment I glance down, he leaps.

The bed jostles beneath his weight, and his hands grip the rafters above. His lean body tenses, the muscles in his arms bulging as he lifts himself up to sit on the dusty old beam above me. It distracts me but only for a second, and then I'm looking down at the pale blonde locks in my fingertips once again.

What the fuck did his perfect pain, perfect pleasure do to me? My fingers twist through the soft blonde hair, but it is most definitely attached to my head. I sit up abruptly, stare into the mirror and come face to face with the green-eyed, blonde haired woman that I apparently am.

"What the fuck, Lighton?" My words come out on a quiet, astounded breath.

"You are welcome," he whispers, staring blankly out the window at something only he can see.

"You can't be a false Alice with red hair. You must be blonde." Kais shakes his head as if he's only ever disappointed in life.

He is good at it. He's really good at being a disappointed asshole.

He's also right. If I'm going to do this, I'll have to do it right.

"What else is expected of Alice?" I finally ask.

Kais looks up to the man perched above us. Lighton arches an eyebrow at him, and the two exchange a look as if they've hidden a thousand secrets away among the silence they share between them.

"She's kind but fierce," Kais tells me. "Smart. And…" His voice trails off, and I'm leaning closer the longer the moment passes without the last little thing on my to do list.

"And?"

Kais doesn't look at me, his big tattooed arms folded firmly in place even as he avoids my stare.

"And she's a virgin," Lighton adds with a dirty smile against his lips.

"What? Why does that matter?" I can't help the defensive sound of my voice, but seriously, why the hell is this even in the legend of Alice Liddell right now? What old man was sitting around jotting down Alice qualifications and double underlined her sexual experience? Or extreme lack thereof.

I'm partly furious that they'd never include this if Alice was an Alec, and I'm also partly furious…because I am in fact a virgin.

But that is not the point!

The point is it shouldn't matter if I've slept with zero men or a whole football team of men. My mind pauses a bit too long on that visual, and then I realize they're both staring at me.

"Are you a virgin?" Lighton asks the question slowly. He looks like he's about to devour me whole right now.

"Why would you ask that? I don't understand what value this holds for our plan." My voice gets higher and higher with every line that rambles out of my mouth. "I'm going to pretend to be Alice, I'm going to marry the King, and I'm going to save two Kingdoms. That's the goal here. My cupcake and the details of how often it gets its icing whipped is none of your business," I shriek the last line out on a trembling voice.

Silence drops into the room.

But Lighton doesn't let it linger long. "Mmm, but really, has anyone tasted your cupcake? Because I, for one, am a big fan of dessert."

Kais's head turns so slowly, cutting a glare toward his friend with newfound aggression. My eyes close, my cheeks blazing with embarrassment.

"You blush like a virgin, Cupcake." Lighton's smirk only grows in his tone.

"That's enough," Kais finally says. "It matters because Alice is the image of innocence. And it matters because the King will find out on your wedding night."

Oh, for outdated standards' fucking sake.

"Can we just get through today? Who's to say his sister will even let this charade go any farther? Let's just get through today, and then we can go from there."

"Well, seeing how we're eight minutes late now, and you're still sitting in bed, I'd say yes, let's get started on getting through today." Kais's features remain impassive as my glare burns a hole through his obnoxiously handsome face.

He's so infuriatingly irritable. I can see the stress in his eyes even if his arrogant posture refuses to show it. He'd be happier—everyone would be happier—if he relaxed a little.

I throw my feet over the edge of the bed, take my time stretching, tilting my head this way and that as I arch my back until each muscle pulls deliciously.

"Done?" Kais licks his lips quickly as if he can rush this along simply by the cutting tone of his voice.

"Should I get dressed first or just prance into the King's castle in my fucking jammies?"

Madison Torrent, False Queen of Wanderlust, Queen in the streets, slob in the sheets.

"Get dressed. Find something innocently blue, and then let's go."

His absurd annoyance with me makes me want to annoy him even more.

"Innocently blue? Is that a color? What if I wore like sad-

ness sapphire or slut red instead? Would the wrong color dress just completely cripple your plan of deceiving the King?"

"Go. Get. Dressed. Fuck, you fight me on everything."

"Because you have no idea how to talk to someone. You just order me around like a little toy soldier. You're shit at guiding and advising. You're a Demander not an Advisor."

"Go." The control he puts into that single word, not shouting it, simply grinding it out like it's all he can do to not shake with anger.

I brush my shoulder against Kais's as I pass, and from above me, Lighton balances his weight, arms out at both sides as he makes his way over to where the beam connects with the attic floor above me. When I climb the stairs, he's right there, trailing at my side as we walk into the mess of fabric that's strung through the enormous room.

"If it means anything, I'd let you be my demented." He bumps his shoulder into mine.

"*Demander*. Demented is…something else entirely."

I truly believe he would though. I don't think anything in the world could make Lighton angry. It's his easy-going attitude that balances Kais just barely.

They're terrible together but good together too.

In a pile of white and pale colored material in the corner, I start to dig. A few articles of clothing have been started. A shirt is here, sleeves missing, ready to be sewn on but not yet assembled. I won't tell Kais, but I secretly love this room. I don't know if a seamstress or maybe a sweet little old lady lived here or what, but this is my dream room. I'd love to just work here in this dusty old place day in and day out.

But I guess that's not in my future. Not for the False Queen.

My fingers catch on a pale blue shirt, and when I pull it out, I find it's a button down made of smooth silk material. Soft fabric slides against my fingertips as I trail them against the garment. Once again, the sleeves haven't yet been attached, but it's long, and with just a few stitches, it could be perfect.

Unless a certain rabbit sneaks up here and finds me making a dress in my free time that isn't really my time to be free.

I look up at Lighton, and he's already crossing the room. He turns on a little overhead lamp near the corner, and there along the wall is a little desk, and perched on top is a black metal sewing machine.

Lighton pulls the wooden chair out with a sharp sound of wood grating against wood. Then he looks to me. He's so... odd but knowing too. Maybe he's aware of more than I give him credit for.

Quickly I sneak over to him, flinching when a floorboard cries out underfoot.

"Better work fast. I can practically hear him checking his watch as we speak."

I smirk at Lighton but take my seat in the little chair. His hand rests against the back of the wooden chair, his warmth lingering against my skin as he watches me get to work. He isn't overcrowding, he's just curious, I guess. I like him watching. It's nice to feel like someone has an interest in my work.

The thin needle is poised and ready, blue thread in place as if whoever was here last was working on the very same project I am now. My bare foot presses to the cool metal of the foot pedal, and in just moments, the machine fires to life. I take my time with the steady bob of the needle. I perfect the cut off arm sleeves, take in the hem on each side, then remove a few buttons and sew up the bottom.

Perfect. Done. That only took...fifteen minutes.

Kais's going to murder me with a spool of thread if another minute ticks by.

As quickly as possible, I stand and pull the worn t-shirt over my head. It hits the floor near Lighton's shoe.

"Oh, okay then," Lighton says with a pleased nod, his attention drifting slowly down every exposed inch of my skin.

I roll my eyes at him as I huff an anxious sigh and start to pull on the dress before I've even fully kicked off my pants. The silk feels so nice against my skin. It caresses in all the right places. When I pull it up my thighs, it glides across them snuggly. My arms slip in, and the shirt I found is now nowhere to be seen.

The backward shirt leaves smooth material hugging my front, with a line of white buttons down the back.

"Can you button the back?" I look over my shoulder at the man lingering just inches away.

A strand of his golden hair falls free, teasing the amber color of his eyes that are locked on the length of my exposed back.

Steady fingers meet my bare spine. A breath catches in my lungs as he runs those fingers at a leisurely pace from the nape of my neck all the way down to nearly the curve of my ass. He's big all over. Lighton's hands feel just as big against my skin. He stops where the fabric meets low against my back. He takes his time, torturing me with each little brush of his fingers against my skin. One by one, he trails up until his palm pushes away the length of my blonde hair, careful to slip it over one shoulder before caressing that shoulder, trailing down, and buttoning the final button.

"There. All done, Cupcake," he whispers against my neck, his beard tickling slightly.

My thighs shift, and I force myself not to lean into his broad chest.

"Thanks." The word is a breathless, pitiful sound, and it

only makes him smirk at me.

"Are you sure you're *all done* because twenty minutes have passed." Kais yells up from the room below in the most condescending tone.

He is so exhausting.

My eyes narrow on the place where I imagine him to be standing on the level below, and a need to piss him off even more burns pettily in my heart.

I look around the endless clothes hanging from lines across the ceiling, at the piles of fabric tossed here and there, colors and fabrics of every kind. And then I see it.

Just what I need. The very image of virginal innocence.

Yes. Just what a virgin needs in her life.

Madison

I wish I could say I wasn't putting effort into how much my hips are swinging as we trail toward the castle. But this morning, I'm channeling my inner Catrice as I stride sensual steps through the forest. Pine needles sprinkle across the dark dirt, casting deep green over the earth, and where the shining glittering mushrooms were last night, only ordinary white fungi remain. The mystery and the appeal of Wanderlust is more of a nightlife. The beauty of the Kingdom of Hearts sleeps during the day only to come alive at dusk.

"You're wearing that just to piss me off." Kais doesn't even look at me and the performance of my swaying hips.

What a waste. My pettiness is insulted.

"What? This old thing?" I cock my head at him, and still he ignores my antagonizing tone.

"You look fantastically fuckable, don't listen to him." The distracted man's appreciating gaze settles on me and me alone as it lowers down my frame.

Kais spins on Lighton, showing just a little hint of that dangerous rage he hides.

"Do not call her fuckable. Don't. Don't even look at her. You two are going to get us murdered. You're going to screw this up before we even step foot into the castle." He takes a slow breath and turns to me, passing a glare down at the black stockings caressing my thighs.

They're sheer, smooth, and nice against my skin. They turn the sweet silk of my nice mid-length dress into a smutty fantasy. The lacy tops of the stockings leave a half an inch of my revealing pale skin showing. Lighton's attention has lingered on that half an inch with nearly every step I've taken this morning.

Honestly, if Kais didn't push and push and push, things would be different. But he just makes me crazy, and that's why things are difficult for us.

"I'm not going to screw this up." I level him with a serious look that matches his own. "I just don't want to be a fucking puppet either. I'm a person, Kais." If he wasn't such a prick all morning, I would be the very image of innocence right now. But I have no problem stooping low to piss him off. I might have an image to protect now, but no one's going to dictate who I'm supposed to be. I've been told I'm weak, sick, and sad all my life. I was told from the very start I can be whoever I want to be in Wanderlust.

And so I will.

"I'm trusting you." Kais's tone is sincere. The anger that usually blemishes his words isn't there.

The simple statement warms me inside and out, and I let go of the tension in my shoulders.

"You can trust me," I whisper back.

For a moment, he and I just stare at one another. Then he

nods slowly, turns on his heels, and starts up the waning boards of the cliffside staircase. My black high heels scuff against the first step, and my palm grips the railing immediately even though I'm only three inches off the ground. I never realized I had such a massive fear of heights, but this daunting staircase has definitely put that fear into perspective.

A big hand pushes against my hip. "You're okay. I got you, Madison."

I nod at Lighton's calming rasping words, and for whatever reason, that simple little hold he keeps on my hip makes the pressing anxiety in my chest ease little by little. My steps start to match Kais's as he trails up the winding back and forth angle of the stairs.

The nerves tumble down in my stomach the closer and closer we come to the top of the cliff. The sound of the waves crashing below and the gentle squawking of the birds overhead aren't even a thought in my head. A new bout of fear and nervousness is storming around my chest.

I'm about to lie to the most important man in the Kingdom of Hearts.

And then I'll marry him.

Chapter Thirteen

Lighton

A mask falls across that gorgeous face of hers the moment she's seated before the King. His study isn't filled with books; there aren't maps or historical documents. It's more of a charming little lovers' den than anything. If the King and his sister were lovers, that is. A long sleek red table sits at the center, surrounded by high arching windows. Deep crimson hearts kiss the middle of each of the shining windows, and they cast a bleeding hue across white walls and the portraits that hang there.

Over the many, many fucking portraits, that stain of red taints each and every one of them. And depicted in each and every one is a golden couple. King Constantine and his bitter better half: his sister.

Instead of books and documents, he has happy little pictures of a woman who wants his crown more than she wants anything else.

And he loves her more than anything else.

They're the strangest non-couple I've ever met.

My thumb brushes back and forth along the silver chain bracelet around my wrist. It's a calming token of who I once was. It grounds me, keeps me focused when my mind starts to wander.

I need to focus today.

I stand stoic at the entry door to the study, concealing my watchfulness as I settle my gaze on the sexy woman who is just now noticing the peculiar number of pictures lining the walls. Yes, yes it is as odd as she's imagining it to be right now.

Madison Torrent might be a fierce little vixen, but she has no idea what she just signed up for.

I wish I could warn her. She's sweet and getting caught up in a bigger issue than what it seems. In my report to the Elder I work for, I'll try my best to protect her.

I can't protect her here though. There are too many dangers, too many sides to try to play. She's only seen Wanderlust's side. Kais's side. The safe side.

More is waiting.

"I'm so pleased you decided to stay, Alice." King Constantine beams at her as her ivory skin blanches impossibly paler.

"Please, call me Madison."

It's the King's turn to blanch at that.

Kais sits quietly at her side, him glaring on one side, the King frowning on the other side, and a scowling Un-Queenly sister leering across from her. It's a lovely, lovely morning, I tell you.

"My brother will call you Alice. And for future dinners, let's be on time going forward. He is a man of importance, and it is incredibly disrespectful to waste his precious time." Konstance's gray eyes narrow into tinier little slits as she gazes at Madison.

"It is alright, Sister." Constantine pats the woman's arm lightly, but it doesn't deter her angry attention. All the gesture does is bring Madison's gaze to the small touch the two just shared.

I smirk to myself, wishing like hell I knew what was slamming through her pretty blonde head right now. But right now, it's easy to see. It's what's always in everyone's head: is the King of Wanderlust fucking his sister?

Is he or isn't he?

Neither of them appears to be too particularly happy, so it's pretty fucking plausible. Constantine looks like the type of guy to *get off* and then get off. Poor fucking Alice.

Huh, poor fucking Madison, I suppose.

My gut twists at that. She's too young to be unhappy. No one knows unhappiness better than I do. That tight feeling in my chest becomes choking again.

I need a drink.

"I'm very sorry for our lateness," Madison says with a tight, pretty smile in place.

Hmm, maybe she is a good pick. She's good at faking happiness and politeness.

"I want to be forward in our plans. I know it might be a strange and premature"—leave it to Constantine to talk about premature, am I right?—"suggestion, but I'd like you to be actively considering the proposal of Queen, Al—Madison."

Madison gives a gentle nod of her head. Long blonde hair shifts against her features, and it kills me to think I took away that sexy red hair. Luckily the blonde will naturally fade away. I'll have to redo the damn magic all over again within twenty-four hours. She's pretty as a blonde though. More innocent looking.

"I don't think it's too forward at all. I'm happy to be here with you, and I'm happy to be considered for your Queen. All I

want is to help our people, Constantine."

At the soft sound of her words, his eyes dilate. You'd think those puffy full lips of hers just uttered the sexiest dirty talk anyone's ever heard. I almost throw up in my mouth as I cling harder to the silence I'm supposed to be holding. It's disgusting how much he gets his rocks off simply from her stroking his political ego.

"He's your King. Please remember to address him as such." Konstance's voice grates through her brother's trance.

"No, I like it. Call me Constantine, please."

Gag.

"I will, *Constantine*." She beams a full smile at him, and it's hard for me to hear anything with all the proverbial dick sucking that's slurping through the room.

Would it be too disruptive if I convulsively vomited all over the floor right now?

A heavy sigh falls out of my lungs, and I don't even realize how loud it is until all four of them look up at me from across the long and daunting table.

Shit, what were they just saying? Did they ask me something?

Their stares linger on me until it's awkward. And I know awkward.

"That a new one?" I point to the portrait closest to me. It's a painting of Konstance in nothing but a ruby red cloak, her long legs peeking out the front, the curve of her breasts teasingly on display while she holds a scepter in one hand, her brother's hand in the other. Her brother oddly stands at her side with a serious look of kingly confidence. My brow pulls low as I try to make sense of the weirdness, but I can't. "It's…nice. I like the…way the cloak covers her pussy just right. Kinky and classy." With my fingers, I give them the A-Okay gesture, and it only makes them glare harder at me.

Nope. Still awkward.

"What is he doing here, Brother?"

"I'm not sure, Sister."

"He's my new advisor. Lighton is really knowledgeable. He's been keeping me up to speed on all details of Wanderlust and your beautiful Kingdom." Madison bites back the smirk in her features as she looks at me, and I swear to God, my dick just got hard.

You know how many people have stood up for me in my life?

None.

And she wouldn't either if she knew what I've done. I used to have this beautiful little girl who looked at me like I was capable of hanging the stars in the sky. She looked at me just like Madison's looking at me right now.

And now I'm just a fucking spy. I'm a traitor just like Kais.

It's worse though. Kais has the support and respect of the rebels. He's my best friend. And not even he knows about my connection to the Elder in Wonderland.

I'm alone in all this.

I swallow hard, and despite the confidence Madison has in me, I want nothing more than to fuck everything up by getting black out drunk again on Rosen.

My gaze shifts to the clock on the far wall. Only twenty minutes have passed. I have a long time before we leave this place and I can really relax again.

Until then, I'll try a bit harder to keep myself from gagging after every smile she gives him, I'll keep my comments to myself, and I'll do my best just to be the watchful spy that no one suspects.

For now.

Chapter Fourteen

Madison

The longer the morning carries on, the more I start to wonder just what the relationship is between Constantine and Konstance. I've seen close twins before. It's a beautiful bond that I can't even begin to understand. It's something I craved sometimes: having a friend that knows you and loves you regardless of anything else.

But this is different.

They don't look to one another in sexual ways. There are no coy glances or lingering touches. It's just…it's like Konstance… wants to be Constantine. I'm fairly certain that's what it is. She wants that power. And maybe the King feels guilty for holding it when it's what his sister so deeply wants.

King Constantine might be obsessed with Alice, but Konstance is obsessed with the crown.

I'm not saying she's evil; that's just crazy. But I grew up with books and movies in place of friends. Between those fictional pages, I've loved a thousand men, met a thousand friends, and I've also met my fair share of villains.

No one spots a villain faster than a book nerd.

And Konstance, she's a villain in the making.

"I just hate the idea of you marrying all alone," she pouts.

My eyes narrow on the strange sentiment. I arch an eyebrow at Kais, but his features are as blank as ever.

"Well, it's a union of two people, so he won't be alone," I say slowly.

The entire arrangement of a wedding is the joining of two fucking people. What in the ever-sibling-loving fuck is turning in her mind right now?

"I meant without me," Konstance snaps sharply.

Of course she did.

"Perhaps you should find a partner of your own, Sister."

"Perhaps I will, Brother." When she mimics his thoughts right back to him, I realize then that this beautiful woman in the deep red gown isn't the Queen of Hearts, and the King isn't the Wonderland King I thought he was.

They're Tweedle-fucking-dee and Tweedle-fucking-dum.

I blink slowly at that realization.

What hole have I thrown myself into where I'm prepared to marry a Tweedle twin? This is going to be more work than I realized. I take a long drink of the cold water as they continue to speak as if the two of them are the only people in the room.

In the Kingdom.

In the world.

"We should arrange something. Today. Someone strong but who won't get in your way. You're not a fan of sharing the lime light." That's for fucking sure. Her brother carries on, "Someone

100

who won't require too much love, you're not the sappy type. Maybe someone who's just cold and a little too broken to really require much attention." Both of them are nodding their blonde heads, and I almost want to scream at what they're concocting together. They're just spewing out ideas of how they can use someone to their benefit.

Is this the way they sat around and spoke of me? Or... Alice, should I say.

"I got it!" Constantine says with an excited snap of his fingers.

I take another slow sip of my water as I imagine myself strangling him with the shining golden crown on his head.

"The Rotter," the two of them both say in perfect unison.

The Rotter? My nose scrunches at the serial killer sounding name alone.

"Who's The Rotter?"

Konstance's red lips curve into a wide smile. "My future husband, of course."

Chapter Fifteen

VII MCM 1197 CXX XVVX 1 277 4884

The Rotter

Agargled choking of words catches in the throat of the man who's pinned like a moth to my desk. It's where I do my best work. It overlooks mossy green forest with the most inspiring view.

I give a lustful little sigh, but it's hard to appreciate it all when he starts to scream again.

"Listen, Ben, I'm not saying you can't rebel. You rebel your Rebel Heart out." I run my finger from the tip of my blade down the thin slicing edge of it. "I'm just suggesting you rebel a bit quieter. At a smaller level. From a distance." I look up at my guest, naked and gagged, tied down at each of the four corners of the steel plate desk. He doesn't nod to me.

A little support, that's all I'm asking for.

It's hard to find compromising rebels any more. They all have too much pride.

Pride is what gets them killed.

The large bat-like wings on my back bristle, catching his attention, making his eyes widen for just a moment. A smile tilts my lips at the sight of his growing fear.

Ben is a wise man. He should be afraid.

"So what do you say, my friend? Do we have a deal?" I pull the dirty cloth from his mouth, and he purses his lips with an angry pinch to his face, preparing to spit at me as they all do.

My leather gloved hand clamps over his mouth, getting up close and personal so the low tone of my voice can really be understood. "Stop drawing the King's attention to yourself. Do. You. Understand?"

I lift my hand, and he immediately screams in my face. "Fuck you, Rotter."

And then my blade slashes across his neck, spewing thick blood over my suit and across my face. My lashes close, and I count to three, lingering there until I'm sure his heart has stopped beating.

They never listen to reason. Every one of them. Too filled with pride to take my offer to let them off with a warning.

I pull the white pocket square from my suit and wipe the blood from my face. The streaks of crimson along the crisp, clean fabric make my eyes widen. I fold it neatly into fours and slip it into the pocket of my trousers to store it away with the others I have. I like to keep them, remember the work I've done from time to time.

I know what that says about me. Keeping bloody towels seems a little…unusual, but we all have our hobbies. It's the little things in life you have to cherish.

Otherwise, you have nothing.

"Mr. Stone, the King has called for you down at the castle." Martha wipes her hands on a dish towel, standing at a distance in the doorway of my office.

"Please tell the King that I am with one of our guests, Martha."

She shifts on her feet, not glancing down once at the dead man pinned to my desk. She's a good housekeeper. She doesn't judge me. Doesn't make a fuss over the messes I occasionally make.

But I can tell when she's nervous.

Not much makes her nervous.

I arch a blood covered eyebrow at her.

"It's just that he said it was urgent. He said…he said that Alice was here."

Alice…

I push out of my bloody jacket and inspect my white shirt. It's clean, nearly bloodless. Acceptable for a formal meeting with the King and his long-awaited Alice.

The former Rebel Heart, Mr. Benjamin Cline, will have to wait to resume our business.

I have a date with an Alice.

A dirty little secret. That's what I am. The King won't tell his little sister how often he meets with me. He'd never dream of telling her about the outcast assassin he pays under the table to get rid of their rebel problems.

That's why I'm so intrigued as I sit at the glossy table across from the pretty blonde woman and the Rebel Hearts' leader himself, Kais St. Croix. I sit here like an equal. And maybe, just maybe, that's why I try extra hard to make them all uncomfortable. I partially want to watch Konstance squirm from my nearness, but I'm also just so damn good at it. Understanding people, finding their weaknesses, and making people uncomfortable—it just comes naturally.

A smile carves at the corner of my lips, and the simple sight of it makes Konstance shiver. You'd think I was a hideous monster instead of the guy she tried to fuck the very first night we met all those years ago when I arrived here.

Before she knew.

With careful care, I remove the leather gloves from my fingers, revealing the black scar that lines my right hand. Konstance peers at the inky wound with big judgmental eyes. I choose to lay my gloves down between her and me, and just as I expected, she inches her chair just slightly away from them.

Another smile slices over my features. "Good morning, my King."

"Rotter." He nods swiftly at me, using the shitty pet name they've all given me.

My gaze shifts to his sister, and I extend my hand as if I'd have the absolute audacity to kiss her boney knuckles. She pulls back from me with a hard line slitting across her lips. "Konstance." The wicked smile against my mouth widens when she flinches at the sound of her name on my tongue, like the words themselves might infect her with my disease.

"Rotter." My name is a snap of syllables from her.

"What was your name before? Why Rotter? I don't understand," the innocent blonde says, her head tilting at me, studying my inky hair, enormous leathery wings, the scar running down the side of my face, and finally the black mark on my hand.

She's beautiful in that delicate way. In that way that you know life will hurt her if given the opportunity. If this were the story of Adam and Eve, this woman wouldn't be innocent Eve at all. She'd be the apple. Shining and untouched. Just waiting to be devoured, and left to rot.

"My name is Alixx Stone, but the name 'The Rotter' outshines me." I keep my words proper, as formal as the upbringing that was drilled into me all those years ago on the surface world.

"Why the Rotter?" Big green eyes shift across my face.

"Because I'm rotting." My hand lifts, splaying my fingers wide to her, and her eyebrows pull together when I motion to the inky black scar. "A terrible disease infected my country long before I came here. I brought that disease with me to Wanderlust."

Her gaze briefly follows the jagged scar that runs down the side of my face and cuts across my throat. That, that is a different story that I've never told a living soul about.

And I know they'll never ask.

"Don't touch him," Kais whispers to her, his head tilting closer to her, his fucking blonde hair mixing with hers like he's better than me. The cocksucker.

I'm bitter. I am. I just refuse to show it.

It's amazing the little things you note when you're no longer able to have them. Just slightly, Kais's arm brushes against the woman's elbow, but neither of them notices. My body would be on fucking fire with nerves and adrenaline if her skin touched mine like that.

"Ever? No one touches you ever?"

I shake my head at her slowly, watching the curiosity glint in her eyes. It's hard to look away from the intrigue she's showing.

"And how many people have caught the…was there a name for it?" She locks her jaw against the hundreds of other questions it seems she wants to ask.

"It was just something that afflicted my country. And luckily I've contained it to only myself."

"So it was something from your past life. Decades ago."

"A century. Over a century ago," I correct.

"Okay. It's not something that happened in Wanderlust

and not one person has caught this…deadly mysterious plague, but everyone continues to fear it."

"Yes."

They fear it. They fear me. I've made myself into an image to be feared too. I can't change my scars, but the sinister wings that shadow my existence only adds to the terrifying image they paint me as.

In this place, you can appear to be anyone you want to be. I want to be exactly who I am inside and out. And I want them to be absolutely clear about that. Hence, the unnerving wings.

Her eyes narrow on me, and I love that dirty challenge in her gaze. Thank the Wanderlust stars I postponed the rest of my meeting today with Ben to be here.

"Let's try to get back on topic, shall we?" Constantine tilts his head to me, and I just barely manage to pull my attention away from her.

But I can't.

"I didn't catch your name." I turn back to her, my interest growing right along with the manic smile pulling across my lips.

"Madison Torrent."

"Alice. Her name is Alice." Konstance interrupts with that shrill voice of hers.

Alice.

I don't know if I believe that, but I'm not a prophet either.

"I was hoping you'd court Konstance. Starting today."

That. That rips my fucking attention right back to him. He should have led with that.

"I'm sorry. You…you want me to court your fucking sister?" The pleasant tone I ask that in seems to go unappreciated.

"Watch your language in front of the ladies, Rotter."

Constantine holds his stern look on me for several seconds, and I choose not to remind him that his lady of a sister tried to taste my cock once upon a time. Until I warned her about my scar, that is.

I was a gentleman and she was…completely fucking disgusted.

Doesn't seem like the right time to mention that tidbit of our history though.

I'll save it for another time.

"Konstance needs a man in her life, and we're considering a fine gentleman such as yourself."

It takes me less than two seconds to read between those lines.

They want someone who they can employ and who they can shove off whenever they like. I get it. Konstance and I would make an attractive, lovely, lovely, miserable fucking couple.

The thing is, whoever puts themselves in the middle of the twins' extremely codependent, screwed up relationship is going to be miserable.

At least this way, I'll have the innocent, corruptible Madison for company.

"I'll do it."

My arm slings up carelessly but with intent onto the table top, and Konstance all but falls out of her chair to keep the distance between her and me. To add a dramatic flair, I cough into my arm, letting the charade carry on for several seconds, and at that, she does get up. She gets up and starts circling the room like she just remembered she wanted to get in a morning's powerwalk. Right this very second.

"You like messing with us." The intriguing woman, Madison, leans forward, her hands brushing over the tabletop, so near mine that it makes me fucking insane.

With my heartbeat drumming and my attention held on the eleven inches separating her fingertips from my palm, I look up at her with the most aloof smile. "I don't know what you mean, Alice."

The name seems to frustrate her immensely, but she does a good job of not showing it, aside from that tiny twitch of her lips. I'll keep that little detail tucked away. Add it to all the details I steal away for my lonely free time.

No one, let me repeat that so we're all clear, *no one* associates with me. No one will risk catching a centuries old disease on the off chance that our arms accidentally brush. So I have plenty of spare time to obsess and drill down to what really makes these people tick.

Take Kais St. Croix for example:

"I hear a large dose of lylacsen has infected our water supply. The drug is harmless, especially in a diluted state, but it is known to cause delightful hallucinations." I watch with big eyes as Kais stiffly lowers his glass from his lips…he pauses for consideration…and then he spews the gulp of water back into the cup with a gasp and cough that sounds through the room for several seconds.

Drugs. Kais St. Croix might run around here like a general, but really, he's an addict. He used to be anyway. And you'd never see that unless you watched every little move he makes. Which is exactly what I do on Monday nights.

Friday nights though, Friday nights are now my Madison Torrent nights. The people here have stopped keeping tabs on time, but I haven't. I will be reserving that special time for her and all the alluring little things that make the woman seated across from me tick.

"Like I said, you like messing with us." Madison arches an—are her eyebrows just the faintest hint of red?

"I do not know what you mean, sweet Alice."

Another fucking twitch of those full lips. Another burst of elation within my chest just from the fact that I know I'm crawling under her skin despite the fact that I haven't touched her.

Nor will I.

"As I was saying, the courtship, as you can imagine, will be a bit unconventional. Please remember to always wear your gloves"—the King's gray eyes look pointedly down at my black leather gloves—"and we will enjoy your company, but of course, be cordial."

"I am nothing if not cordial, my King." Fuck cordial. Cordial is for people who have to look at their peers day in and day out and typically give a shit about what thoughts they think of you.

The King smiles happily with the arrangement he's made. It's entirely screwed up that I know I'll be courting a woman who, had she hired a better assassin than myself, would rather see me dead. It's also a little odd that I know I'll be courting her as well as her brother, because you don't get one without the other.

Not that I care to have either one of them. But, it's a moderately lonely life I live. I have the free time, why not use it wisely? A favor for the King is always good.

But wait, it gets better.

"You'll be spending a fair amount of time with myself as well as my…*betrothed*, Madison."

I can't help the manic smile that pulls across my lips as I look up at my Friday night.

"I'm sure Alice and I will get along just fine."

Her eyes narrow into thin slits just as those lips of hers do exactly what I knew they would.

Thank the Wanderlust I showed up to meet the sweet, corruptible Madison.

110

Madison

The King closed the door on me to speak with his advisors. I can't be too upset about it since Alixx and Lighton were both shown the door as well. The three of us linger in the hall while the sound of Konstance's voice grows louder and louder.

"If he touches me, if I'm plagued from all of this—"

"You won't be. Calm down. You want someone who knows their place. Rotter knows. Rotter will not get in your way, Sister."

The two voices mingle together, and I don't hear a single word from Kais, but the man isn't exactly the talkative type in front of his King.

Smart for a guy playing both sides.

My head tilts closer to the door, and just as I'm listening intently, a big palm slams firmly next to my face. I blink at the sudden rattling of the door, casting my gaze to the man crowding my space.

"It isn't polite to eavesdrop, my Alice." His gloved hand stays there, right in my line of sight while his chest nearly brushes mine.

Peculiar black wings shadow the sharp angles of his face, nearly hiding the scar that runs up to meet the corner of his left eye. The wings are bat-like. They're not pretty, but they match his hair and make his eyes seem brighter.

Alixx is…strangely beautiful in a flawed way.

He's so damn cocky though. He must really believe he's the only person to come into this world with a sickness. Maybe he is. Until me that is.

And I know his secret: he isn't diseased at all. Sure, he was. At one time, he obviously was. And maybe he truly believes that he still is.

But Wanderlust cured me, so I know it cured him as well.

I didn't have friends in school. I had books and I had my homework, and I threw my lack of a social life into my grades. A simple glance at a history book will tell you that plagues don't kill at a slow impossible pace. He'd never make it over a century with just a jagged blemish on the back of his hand. Whatever disease he had in the surface world isn't in him now.

I lean into him, cutting his breath off immediately with the nearness of my mouth to his. He's tall, a few inches taller than myself, making me tilt my chin up to breath my words against his lips.

"I already have one bossy male in my life. I don't need another."

His breathing increases visibly just from how close I'm standing to him. It feels oddly good to give him a dose of his own medicine. How does he like being the one played with?

Dark eyebrows lift as he stares stunned at me, his green eyes becoming wide but lust-filled as he glances down at the nearness of our mouths.

"Madison, don't touch him," Lighton whispers from somewhere behind me.

I keep my attention held on Alixx and the devilish gleam in his gaze.

"What game are you playing, Alice?"

He is good at his infuriating games though. Because I can't fucking stand him and I just met him.

My lips thin, and I know he's doing the Alice name to piss me off. Neither of us moves. We keep the challenging space between us, letting a fire blaze between the small spaces that separate our bodies. It really is a game in this moment. A game that neither of us knows the rules to and neither of us is willing to lose.

"I don't know what you mean, Alixx." The use of his name seems to have the opposite effect from when he uses Alice on me.

The darkness of his pupils dilates, and he looks at me with so much heat in his emerald eyes that my breath catches, making me forget that I really am playing a game with this strange, beautiful man. I wanted to piss him off and make him crazy, but it's a dangerous game it seems.

I'm only making myself crazy. Making the both of us crazy.

"Listen to your rabbit friend, sweet Alice. *Don't* touch me." A splatter of red along his white collar pulls at my attention, but what's more demanding is the way he glances down to my lips once more as if he's memorizing the way my mouth looks so close to his, fantasizing about how it'd feel if my lips pressed to his, my body wrapping around his…

It's a dangerous, dangerous game I'm getting lost in.

"Let's get one thing straight. Your fearmongering doesn't work on me. Don't feed me your lies, Alixx. Don't mess with me the way you mess with everyone else, and you and I will be just fine."

I should step back. I should back down, and I should show some sort of formal distance between myself and the man who will someday be my brother-in-law.

But I don't. Just like *The Rotter*, I'm sheltered. I haven't really felt the heat of a man's body...*ever.* Not one I was attracted to. Not one with such defined shoulders and beautiful eyes and taunting lips.

"I can't make any promises, Alice. But believe me when I say, I'm not lying. And on the off chance that I'm telling you the truth: Do. Not. Touch. Me." The sad but angry way he says that is what makes me snap.

Like I said, I make bad decisions.

And I'm about to make one more.

I just can't take the empty sadness in Alixx Stone's green eyes. He can mask it with indifference and pettiness all he wants, but it's there. He's being eaten alive with sadness.

And he doesn't even know it.

My gaze locks with his, and with slow intent, I lean forward, pressing my hands to his black vest, to the hard planes of his chest as I shift up on the toes of my high heels. Every muscle in his body stiffens. He doesn't move an inch. All that cocky masculinity is gone the very moment my hands land on his body. And then I brush my lips faintly against his.

I tear the façade of The Rotter away just like that. It's empowering, in a way, to see how easily his charade of a personality can be torn away. Whatever wall this man built around his little black heart just came crashing down all because a virgin woman had the balls to kiss him chastely on his ever-taunting lips.

114

The gentleness of his hands against my hips makes my fingers fist harder into his shirt, pressing my lips more firmly against his until everything I feel and everything I breathe is Alixx Stone.

"Shit," Lighton whispers so quietly it barely registers in my mind.

That single word pulls him away from me. Alixx steps back so suddenly I stagger from the amount of faith I had apparently put in his body supporting mine. He turns away from me, giving me the span of his inky wings while running his hand over his face slowly.

All I see is his confused but blatant frustration.

Then he vanishes right before my very eyes.

I blink and he's gone. The long gold and cream-colored hall looks wider without him in front of me.

"What—" What the fuck?

Lighton pulls at my shoulder, forcing me to look up into his amber eyes. He searches my face, his gaze analyzing every single detail while he holds me at arm's length.

"Where did he go?" I peer past him, but the quiet corridor is empty aside from us.

"Why did you do that? Are you out of your mind?" Lighton pulls me a little closer, leaving a meager amount of space between our bodies.

"Where did he go? He just…disappeared?"

"He's been here a long time. Second to Kais. His magic is more advanced." Lighton keeps his hands firmly on my shoulders while he looks at every inch of me carefully.

The door creaks open, and I jump from the sound of it. Lighton slowly releases his hold on me when we're met with stern eyes. How can the most beautiful blue eyes be so…angry? All of the time.

115

Kais looks from Lighton to me. He carefully dissects the two of us, our closeness and everything in between, as if he can decide if Lighton's deflowered me right here against the King's door without anyone ever noticing.

"This is taking longer than expected. I'll meet you two back at my house." Kais cuts his attention up to Lighton before adding, "No house guests tonight."

Lighton makes a face as if he wouldn't dream of it. But the way Kais stares him down tells us that they both know Lighton would in fact dream of it.

"I don't like this. Honestly, how do you even know her number won't turn black soon? She hasn't even been here a day, Constantine," the voice shrills loudly, and Kais pulls the door shut in an instant without so much as a goodbye slipping through.

Lighton shifts on his heels, turning to me with a smile pulling at his lips. "I need a drink. What about you?"

I came to Wanderlust and was told I'd marry a king. Instead I'm setting out to get drunk with a rabbit...

It's odd how much more appealing that sounds. I don't look back at the King's door as I walk down the quiet hall with the rambling rabbit.

We don't get drunk though. We don't even make it back to Kais's house.

A glittering white waterfall shimmers down to a pool of natural water. It glints with the promise of something magical infused in the water that Lighton's stripping down in front of. Cat and, to my surprise, Brody are here. Naked. Swimming and laughing and touching coyly beneath the water. Lighton's gray shirt lies in the dirt near a pine tree while he takes his time unbuttoning his jeans. I can't help but watch him blatantly. The small of his back has two perfect dimples. Higher up, curving muscle tone etches

lines across his back; his arms never flex, but his biceps are curved with shadows of strength. Every single part of him is big.

And so he reminds me as he lowers his jeans.

He turns to me with a small smirk, and it's incredibly hard for me to keep my attention focused on his mouth and his eyes and just his handsome face.

"Come in with us." His gaze trails so slowly down my body that I feel his attention flittering across my skin.

"I do happen to remember the last time I was naked in shimmering water with you, and it wasn't the best moment of my poor-decision-making life."

"Poor decisions or romantic memories?"

"Definitely poor decisions." I nod to him, and his smile only grows.

Honestly, I want those poor decisions. I want to be a girl who makes memorable mistakes. I want the thrill of living. The good, the bad and the ugly.

And those 'poor Lighton decisions' I made yesterday—those would fall under the good. The very good.

"You were naked with Lighton. Do tell." Cat swims gracefully to the edge of the water, resting her glistening arms on a smooth rock as she peers up at me. "Did you lick his waffle abs?"

My lips part as I try to speak, but I don't know what to say to that. "Waffle abs?"

Lighton sinks down into the clear water, and it glimmers brighter around his waist for just a few seconds before dimming faintly.

"You know. The type of abs you want to pour syrup over and lick across every single divot of yumminess and hope and pray that those calories go straight between your thighs." Cat's lavender eyes gleam like a kitten spotting a mouse.

Being the arrogant ass that he is, Lighton pushes his big palm across his chest, raining water down his stomach in a way that highlights the very thing that Cat was describing.

Waffle abs indeed. Definitely something I'd want between my thighs.

"Cat wouldn't lick any part of me."

"I would. If your personality matched those abs, I definitely would. It's a shame, really." Cat smiles as she floats leisurely on her back, displaying the perfect curve of her breasts from beneath the water.

Brody sneaks up behind her, wrapping his arms around her stomach and pulling her against his chest. She smiles as her sharp nails skim over his knuckles. The proper gentleman and the smutty cat. They are an interesting pair. I bet Cat makes memorable mistakes.

Do I really need any more bad choices in my life though?

"Come swim with us," Lighton says again.

His shoulders are relaxed, his gaze sweet but not hooded like they were this morning.

"I don't know what kind of drug this is. This isn't really my thing." I try not to sound like a complete judgmental good girl.

"It's not like last night. Rosen is really strong. It's different. It feels more like a Tylenol. It makes your body feel better, your muscles relax. It's good for you, trust me."

It's good for you. Really?

Sure, maybe I've never met an actual drug dealer before, but that does sound like something they'd say.

"Really, trust Light, he was a doctor after all." Brody keeps his hungry gaze fixed on Cat, but he sounds completely honest right now, even if what he said astounds me.

That's not true. Is it?

"That's a lie." Cat rolls her eyes. "He was a stripper on the surface. Remember the waffle abs, Maddy." Cat hisses like it's a secret she's just willing to share with me.

"I wasn't a stripper." Lighton smirks, but Cat just talks over his denial.

"You know who else has waffle abs?"

I shake my head.

"Strippers," she stage whispers.

"I was *not* a stripper."

"He was," she mouths behind his back, shaking her head hard.

"He was also a performer in Cirque Du Soleil. Not one of the sexy acrobats though. A clown of course." Brody's smile grows larger as Lighton narrows his eyes on his friend.

"I was *not* a clown."

"Well, maybe not professionally." Brody shrugs his bare shoulders, and Cat cackles an adoring laugh that makes me smile as well.

I lower myself down at the edge of the water, pulling my shoes and sheer tights off with little grace before slowly sinking my feet into the warm glittering cove.

Lighton wades closer, the water lapping up against his hard stomach with every step he takes.

"You do trust me." There's a hint of a smile on his lips, and my body tingles where the glitter coats my skin. It's the most relaxing sensation around my feet and ankles.

"How could I not trust a stripping clown who has a doctorate?"

Another small smile peeks out beneath his scruffy beard.

His hands slice back and forth in the water for just a few

seconds, and then he moves slowly closer, watching me intently as he seems to think out his next move. My body thrums with the thought of him touching me. His palms skim along the surface, and my skin tingles even more when he takes my foot in his hands. His fingers knead and press perfectly along the arch of my foot.

"Careful, he was a happy endings masseuse too," Cat whispers just loud enough to make Lighton shake his head at her.

"That would be a masseur actually." Lighton arches a pale eyebrow at her, but then he backtracks. "I don't know that because I was one…"

"Sure." Cat mockingly nods in agreement.

It's then that I realize all his strange wording has stopped since this morning. He just corrected someone else's word choice.

And he was right.

His little ticks are just calm energy now.

"You're sober right now, aren't you?" I ask.

He gives my ankle a slow roll of his wrists, massaging just right, before skimming his palms higher up my calf. Warm water trails down my skin. A little higher and a little higher he roams, and I can't help but wonder if he'll be working the tension out of my G-spot if he keeps sneaking up my leg like this.

"Unfortunately, yes." His jaw grinds together just slightly, his attention lost and a little too far away.

"I like you sober," I whisper just to him.

He peers up at me with the most beautiful warm brown eyes.

"You're the only one, Cupcake." He swallows hard before speaking again, "I hate who I am when I'm drunk, and I hate the memories of who I used to be when I'm sober." The sadness held in those beautiful eyes rips through my chest.

Slowly I slide down off the bank, slipping down until the

water seeps into my dress, sticking to my thighs like a second skin, and then I'm standing before him, his hands lightly touching my arms, but he's unsure of where to touch me now that I'm just inches from him.

We study each other for several passing seconds.

"Why'd you kiss the Rotter?" he finally whispers.

"You kissed Rotter?" Cat gasps like that's the most scandalous thing the naked woman has ever heard. "Well, what Lighton really means then is why'd you kiss Rotter and not him. Jealousy is not your best color, Light."

Lighton glares over at the cat woman but pulls his curious gaze back to me.

This is really a hot topic for him. For the first time, it seems Lighton is...frustrated.

"You held me in your arms last night. I was naked in your arms, Lighton." I ramble the thoughts out as fast as they come, and his eyebrows lift high at the sound of my honesty. My arms fold across my chest, and he follows the motion, attention lingering on the curve of my breasts. His distracted attention only infuriates me even more. We shared a really sexy moment. A drunken sort of moment, but really it was all there. Our attraction was immediate. He could have marked that one big thing off my bucket list, and I knew he'd do it right.

But he was drunk. And so was I.

He isn't the type of guy I'd want to forget in a drunken night. That's what breaks my heart when I think of how much he misses out on in his own life.

"If you'd have been sober, maybe things would have been different." I stare up into his tragically beautiful brown eyes. He studies me for a moment longer.

"So you won't kiss me unless I'm sober?" I feel like I can

see his little hamster wheel spinning, but the hamster has long since fallen off.

I roll my eyes at his train of thought. It isn't about kissing him. It's about wanting to want him, but he's checked out. I can't want someone who isn't here. He doesn't want to be here; he wants to feel lost. Numb. I don't even know what, but he doesn't want to feel all the things in life I want to feel.

And I want it. I want love and lust and everything in between. I have a real shot at life now, and I'm not wasting it on someone who isn't here for that.

"I'll meet you back at Kais's." Just before I turn away from him, his lips part like he'll say more about it, but he doesn't.

"I have an errand to run, but I'll see you tonight."

We stare at one another for a long moment.

I know when I see him tonight it won't be like this. He won't be the smart, funny, sexy man who's standing before me.

That man will be gone.

And that's the problem.

Chapter Seventeen

Lighton

The migraine cracking through my skull is an appreciated distraction from all the other things clouding my thoughts tonight.

Madison kissed someone riddled with an ancient plague, but my escapism is too much for her.

I heave a heavy sigh as I wait for the signal. A line of thick pine trees shadows me. I stand on the Kingdom's line. Another three feet and I'd be in Wonderland. I'd just have to make it through the invisible burning barrier the Elders put in place to keep newcomer scum like myself out.

I can see it. From time to time, when the moonlight is bright enough, I can see the shield of magic that glints between Wanderlust and Wonderland.

They did a good job, really. No one has ever passed from our Kingdom into the Dismay Forest.

Except for me.

I wish I knew why he picked me. I guess I looked like a good guy at the time. I'm a mess though, inside and out.

And he's starting to notice.

I don't want to give my report tonight. Elder Liddell and I have an agreement though. I pass along the most trivial of information to him, and he lets me pass through Dismay Forest to enter the surface world once a month.

To visit my little sister who doesn't even know I'm there.

It's the one time I make sure I'm sober. And now Madison wants that to be a permanent thing for me.

Sobriety.

Sounds painful.

The burning barrier flashes, gleaming with a wave of white magic before shuttering out. It's the smallest flicker of light.

That's the signal.

I take three slow steps over the line that divides the two Kingdoms.

Now all I have to do is tell the man who's been waiting centuries that Alice has arrived.

I'll risk my arrangement with him by lying. I can't tell him she's a fake even though it'll get her as well as myself in trouble soon enough. Keeping her secrets should tell me that I'm in over my head with this woman. I should consciously realize that. But I don't.

Maybe I really am crazy.

Chapter Eighteen

Madison

They said time does not exist in Wanderlust.

They lied.

It's been exactly three days, and I haven't seen the King or his sister since he basically asked me to go steady and then shoved me out of his life.

And for three days, Lighton has been exactly as I knew he would be.

"Why so glum, chum?" He hangs upside down before me, his legs holding himself to the rafters above my bed. Strands of his golden hair pull free and waft around his face as he rocks back and forth with a slow smile cutting across his handsome face.

Here we go again.

"The King is avoiding her." Kais spreads his long legs wide from the chair next to my bed.

"Wow, really hit the dick on the head with that one."

Lighton nods at his friend who now has a disturbed look crossing his face.

"I think you mean nail."

"No, I think I mean dick." Lighton continues to nod and swing from above.

I wonder how much long-term damage all his forgetting tactics are doing to his beautiful mind. God, I hope Brody was lying when he said Lighton was a doctor.

A knock sounds on a door far, far away.

Kais glances down the stairs. Without another word, his image fades away in a matter of half a second. Then with a popping sound, he's gone.

"He can disappear too?"

"Of course he can. Kais was the first newcomer to Wanderlust. He's the only one of us who was welcomed in the Kingdom of Wonderland. They thought he was a random anomaly. Then Rotter showed up, and they did not like that. That was a long time ago though."

"How long have you been here?"

He tilts his head this way and that, making it more of a strange gesture as he hangs upside-down.

"About a year."

"And you can't disappear?"

"No, but I can—" He pauses a little dramatically as he smiles at me. And then…he too disappears. In a flash, he comes right back into view in the same place.

"You just disappeared…" I lift my hands at my side, but he shakes his head at me.

"No, Kais and Rotter—they can teleport short distances. I can vanish, turn invisible, but I can't physically travel anywhere

with my magic." He kicks off from his place, and with a jostling fall, he lands onto the small mattress at my side.

I do note that it's a sort of acrobatic move involving a small flip. Something very Cirque Du Soleil-ish that I'm going to choose not to comment on at the moment.

Who was Lighton before Wanderlust?

He shifts, settling in and stealing all of my attention. I hate how much my body loves his closeness. His warmth sears into me as he crosses his arms behind his head and really gets comfortable.

"Any…plague like rashes come up yet?"

My eyes hurt by how hard I roll them.

"No. And they're not going to. Alixx doesn't have the plague."

"Maybe. Or maybe you're immune. You're the legendary Alice after all. Your story can't end before it's even begun." His eyes close. I stare at the side of his pretty face like I can glare a hole through that empty hamster wheel if I stare hard enough.

"I'm not Alice."

"Not yet. When you marry, you'll have to change your name just like I change your sexy hair." He absently pushes his fingers through my hair, and my morning red locks turn blonde so easily it makes me want to scream.

In Wanderlust, you can be anyone you want. Unless you're me. Then you're fucked into being innocent Alice.

"Who do you think I would be if I wasn't pretending to be Alice?" I curl in against his side, but I keep a small amount of distance between us. His long fingers continue to stroke through my hair, and he glances at me. He looks at me so closely it's like he's just now seeing me, finding every part of me exposed to him.

"I don't know what you mean."

"Like in Wonderland. The storybook. If this were Wonderland, Kais would be the white rabbit. The twins would be Tweedledee and Tweedledum. Cat would be Cheshire. I…don't have a clue who Alixx would be."

"Who does that make me?" Lighton asks quietly.

"You're the March Hare."

His gaze shifts, his hands halting, strung through my hair while his eyes widen with sad realization.

"The crazy one. Damn. And here I hoped I'd be the dodo." The humor in his voice is more sad than anything.

"We can change our story at any time, Light." There's a gentleness in my voice, and I scoot just slightly closer to him.

His lips tilt up at one side with a half-smile that's barely holding in place.

"Sure." He nods to me and falls back against my pillow without another word.

"If I weren't pretending to be Alice, would I be the Hatter? The *Hattress*?" I lean closer, pushing my chest against his side to try to remind him that I'm here and to get his nonsensical happiness to return.

Laughter rumbles from his chest, and I'm surprised how easy it is to get him to laugh right now. And then I realize it's mocking.

"You wouldn't be the Hattress, Cupcake."

"Why not? You saw my dress I made. I'm great at that stuff. Is it because I'm not crazy enough?"

"You're definitely not crazy enough." He doesn't look at me as his eyes close slowly, a smile still pulled across his full lips.

"Maybe I could be though."

"You're not." He ignores me until I shove at his arm, push-

128

ing his big body until he rocks against my side.

"I could be. If I had a real choice, I could be whatever I want to be. Crazy or not." My lips purse, and I don't know why I'm so serious about this right now.

But suddenly, so is he.

He turns, shifting until he's leaning over me, his big hand clasping over my arm as he stares furious eyes into mine.

"You don't want that. You don't want to be like me, Madison. Be Alice. Be *anyone* else. But don't be like me."

My breath catches. He holds me there, pinning me in place for just a moment longer before he leaps over me, jumping from the bed and slamming his shoulder into Kais's as he goes. He's downstairs and out of sight in a matter of seconds.

Kais stares after the man before letting it go, it seems. In his hand, a bouquet of glittering white roses overflow from a vase, and my eyes widen at the sight of them.

"Everything okay?" Kais sets the vase down at my bedside table, and he lingers there until I stand up and push my white shirt down over my black pajama shorts.

"It's fine. You got flowers?" I touch the alluring rose petals, pulling it close to inhale the floral scent but also keeping a little distance because I have no fucking clue if all the pretty things in this Kingdom are as dangerous as they are beautiful.

"They're from the King."

I pause, glancing up to the handsome tattooed man at my side.

Kais folds his arms, but I can see the impatience in his face.

"Open the card," he snaps the order out, and I narrow my eyes at his tone alone. "Please. Please open the card." The flattest, most half-attempted of all attempted smiles pulls across his lips.

It's something sinfully sexy when a man covered in ink gives you a genuine smile. I feel robbed by the half-assed attempt he's making right now.

I roll my eyes at him and slowly open the small white card.

"It says, 'My Dearest Madison, it would be my absolute pleasure if you could please join me for tea in the royal garden this evening. Yours Forever Truly, Constantine Phillip Thomas Doire III.'" Of course he's the third. The little numbers at the end of his name shouldn't feel as pretentious as my mind is making them out to be, but I just can't help it.

"Great!" Kais is all but clapping right now because the King remembered I existed after three days passed.

Are we sure the guy's obsessed with me? It's not like I'm crying from lack of attention, but Constantine is a terrible number one fan.

Or maybe he was just obsessed with the idea of having me. That sounds painfully more accurate.

"Great," I say with much less enthusiasm.

"Okay, now that you're back in," Kais starts, his eyes alight with excitement and plotting. *Back in* because there were a few days there where I was very much on the out. Asshole. "There are a few things we need to take care of before they get us into some trouble."

My arms cross, but Kais doesn't notice my annoyance one bit.

"Excuse yourself from dinner—"

"Tea," I correct flatly, but he's already carrying on with his plotting.

"Excuse yourself, and then I need you to sneak down to the lower level of the castle."

"The dungeon. You mean the dungeon?"

"Well, some would call it that, sure."

"Don't sugarcoat. You're asking me to treasonously snoop through the castle and then lurk on down to the fucking haunted dungeon."

"It's not haunted. You're being ridiculous."

"What's in the dungeon?"

"In the *lower level*"—a pointed look is thrown at the feet of my pettiness—"is a door created by an Elder. Through the door is a trigger switch. The switch was created to allow people to enter Wanderlust. We don't want that. We don't want anyone else coming through until you're wed."

I pause, thinking through what he just told me until something clicks.

"Because you're afraid the real Alice will show up."

"It's a possibility, yes." His blue eyes hold mine.

"Why wouldn't you want the real Alice, Kais?"

He continues to keep his serious, unyielding look in his gaze.

"We have you. The outcome will be the same except you're a sure thing. You're here now, we don't know when the real Alice will arrive, but you're here now. And you're on our side."

He wants someone he can control. He must see the disgust in my features because for once, he comes a little closer, giving me one of the very few genuine looks of kindness in his eyes.

"Cat told you I was on the winning side of the American Civil War. I was on the right side of history." His gaze is vacant as his palm skims lightly down the inside of my wrist. His words are so gentle it hurts my heart just from the sound of it. "What a lot of people don't remember about the Civil War is there was no winning or losing side in the middle of it all. It was a bloody massacre. War has a price. An incredibly high price. I don't want that

131

here. I don't want a war for this realm. If I have my own Alice, if I have you, I know that things will progress amicably between the two Kingdoms."

The lost look in his sea blue eyes is all I need to understand what he's saying. He's always so cold and angry. I want to curl up against him when he shows me the gentleness inside him.

A little part of me begs for me to ask him what will happen if things don't go according to plan though. What will happen to the False Queen if things go wrong? Will he continue his fake life of playing sides? Or will he pick a side?

Will he pick me?

All these anxious questions burn up my throat, but I don't ask a single one. Kais is determined. He's smart. He's thought of all the possibilities.

I just have to follow orders for once, and we'll all have the life we want in the end.

"Okay, tell me again where the switch is."

The Rotter

*I*n a flash of Wanderlust, I'm four stories in the air, sitting on the ledge of Kais St. Croix's highest window. But it isn't enough. Too many strung up clothes and colorful cloths hang from the ceiling, blocking my view of my beautiful Friday night.

Her long legs shift from where she sits across the room, but I can't see an inch higher.

A frustrated puff of air slices through my lips, and with a quick, halfcocked plan, I disappear right inside. The drilling, even sound of a sewing machine running fills the quietness. Silent steps, meant for silent kills, lead me closer to her. Long blonde locks hang halfway down her back, her head tilted low as she passes her white material beneath the quick needle. She's so focused, so determined right now.

Her lips purse as she comes to the end of the cloth, and I'm reminded immediately of how soft her mouth felt against mine. Never in all the hundreds of years that I've existed has my cock ever gotten hard from something as mundane as needle work, but there's a first time for everything, I suppose.

My head tilts down just behind her, letting my mouth come close to her ear as I watch like the stalking fucking predator that I am.

"Any worrisome rashes, sweet Alice?"

She understandably shrieks. I get that reaction a lot.

Sewing goes askew, chair scrapes, she herself goes toppling backward, chair and all. Fucking woman is a bit less graceful than I originally gave her credit for.

At the very last second, my hands grip the back of her wooden chair, bracing her just before she collides with the floor. I stare into pale, olive green eyes. It's the purest green. Not a hint of darkness. Easter green.

And then her fist darts out.

Understandably so.

My fingers grip her wrist just before she lands her poorly executed punch. Christ, did no one teach this girl how to defend herself?

Probably the lack of a father figure with this one. I tally up all the little things I can string together about the woman I'm still holding just an inch above the ground.

Probably a lack of confident men all together in her life.

"What the hell are you doing here, Alixx?"

The smile that curves my lips suppresses the groan that I hide so well every time she says my name.

Who says a plagued man's name?

No one.

Fucking. No. One.

134

It's like they all think a curse will strike them down if they so much as show me any resemblance of humanity.

"Just wanted to make sure your limbs aren't falling off. Checking to make sure your nose is still attached."

"That's a myth of leprosy, and you don't have leprosy, Alixx." Those green eyes narrow with a hard glare in her gaze.

"Maybe I wanted to make sure your pretty mouth didn't fall off then."

"You're making house calls because you thought my mouth might have mysteriously turned into a gaping hole in the last three days?"

"I thought it was a real gaping hole before we kissed, but it does sound like a serious possible side effect, my Alice. The plague will do that from time to time, I hear."

"Get this through your arrogant skull: you don't have the plague, Alixx. You're one hundred percent entirely normal."

"Normal is a very hurtful thing to call someone."

Her glare turns murderous on me, but I do note that she's not pushing out of my arms as I hold her, careful not to touch her shoulders from around the wooden chair. I'm still smirking down on her when the very distinct sound of a blade unsheathing scrapes through the room.

"What the hell are you doing here, Rotter?"

That. Now that is a welcoming I'm used to.

The sharp point of a blade slips under my chin, and he forces my attention up to him, my glinting gaze still smirking when I look up at the King's most trusted fucking advisor. The one and only secret leader of the Rebel Hearts. And the only man who can get this woman killed before her life has even begun here.

"Mmm, you here to punish me, Daddy?" I tip my head back to press his blade into my throat.

A cold glare from him is the only reaction. It's like he gets called daddy every day and my little sentiment isn't even appreciated.

The asshole.

"Let her go." He nods to the woman I'm sweetly holding up, but who am I to question the demands of the King's advisor.

I release her, and the chair bangs hard against the floor, causing a curse to snap from Madison, her eyes passing me over to glare at the man who gave the order.

With his sword still at my throat, I shrug a small *I did everything I could* gesture and it only makes her lips thin even more.

Kais offers her his hand, and her small palm slips into his, sending a strange flit of jealousy through my veins just because of the casual touch. Thanks to the blade against my throat, I stay casually seated there at their feet. I tilt my head slowly, letting the blade cut the smallest slice into my throat as I wait with blatant patience for him to finish his little protector act.

The little sting of pain calms me, grounds me.

"Care to remove that sword, my friend? Wouldn't want Rotter blood poisoning the blade, would you?" I arch my neck, letting the blade scratch a little more into my flesh, cutting into me just enough that I can feel the warmth of my own blood sliding down my skin.

Completely grounded.

"Kais, stop, you're hurting him," Madison says, and I can't help but smile wider as Kais grimaces harder.

It's not every day I meet someone who pities me. I never knew pity was something I was missing in my long endless life until this very moment.

"Listen to Alice. You're hurting me, Mr. St. Croix."

Both of them curl their lips at me at the same time.

They just make it so damn easy.

"He came to see if a centuries old plague had killed me in my sleep or not." She crosses her arms beneath her breasts, and the loose fitted shirt she's wearing doesn't stop my gaze from traveling her curves.

"Why did he touch you?" Kais's blade pushes just a bit harder against my wind pipe, his jaw twitching as he looks to her.

"No. *I* did not touch *her*."

The truth is in the details. *Give your protector the details, Madison.*

I wait patiently to hear if she'll lie to her boyfriend or not. When she says nothing, I decide I'll just push him a bit more since I'm already here. Without a sound, I vanish from my spot Kais was so intent on pinning me to. I slip in behind her, my fingers toying with the ends of her pale hair as I walk a slow, predatory circle around her.

"I'd never be so rude as to touch a woman without her permission. You of all people should know that I'm a respectable man among so many traitors, Kais."

He turns swiftly, his blade swings up, and I vanish with a crackling sound stinging the air, leaving behind the soft feel of her blonde locks. I reappear directly in front of her, reveling in the breathy gasp that leaves her full lips. My fingers brush along her hair, almost slipping it back behind her ear but not quite.

Another slash of that angry blade and I'm forced to disappear once again.

I smile to myself as I look down on them, Kais turning swiftly to seek me out, her looking around slowly in a more hesitant and almost wistful way.

God, I hate how vividly I remember her lips against mine.

I thought the only thing in the world that I wanted was

to be touched, but now I'm finding it's an incredible torture to remember something you'll never have again.

I drift down with all the magic I possess. My eyes meet hers, my body poised upside down as I lower myself until my lips brush just gently against her ear.

But I can't fucking help myself. My mouth grazes the shell of her ear. I whisper just quietly enough that Kais won't turn toward us and ruin the perfect little moment between a man named the Rotter and a girl who most definitely is not the destined Alice. I like the way her chest rises and falls heavily when I'm near. It's like the tiny little touches that spark me to life affect her as much as they do me.

"I'll see you tonight, my Alice." I'm tempted to press my lips to her cheek, her throat, between her thighs, anywhere she'll fucking let me. But I don't. I play nice.

For now.

Chapter Twenty

Madison

That night, a lively amount of laughter fills the cool evening air. None of it's mine, but Tweedle and Twattle seem to be having a lovely double date.

Alixx and I are just the extras.

Constantine places his palm over my knuckles on top of the small dining table that someone has positioned here in the most romantic setting beneath the stars, among the thousands of glittering white roses, across from the most handsome man who's ever infuriated me to the point of passion.

What in the tweedle fuck is wrong with me?

Alixx leans over the table as Constantine and Konstance share another burst of cackling amusement. "What do you say you and I find a closet somewhere and play that game seventy minutes in heaven?"

"It's seven. Not seventy."

"Well, I don't know what kind of low expectation Kais has set for you, but what I had planned needed at least an hour," he whispers just low enough that the King's sister who's placed a good three feet between her chair and his can't hear him.

"There's no low expectations." I smile politely when Constantine shifts his distracted attention over to me for just the smallest amount of time. "There's none. There's zero expectation."

"Zero." His gaze cuts to his King, my betrothed, before sliding back to me. "That is fascinating. I guess I just don't find you to be as innocent as everyone else does."

He infuriates me but he's so intriguingly different I just can't help but play into the palm of his hand. All he wants is a reaction. And I give that to him time and time again.

And I hate it every single time.

His features remain impassive, but I can see that little arrogant shine of taunting amusement. I shift in my seat and force myself not to antagonize him. I just have to get through this night. I just have to make it a little longer before I can excuse myself.

"I was clearly the favorite." Konstance smirks at her brother.

"Mom always said we were identical and so was her love for us."

"That was a lie to make the less favorite feel better." Konstance sends another shrill of laughter after her own words, and Alixx physically flinches from the sound of it.

"You were not her favorite." It's a half-smile he passes his sister, and I just now notice how quickly she's going through the bottle of Rosen Alixx brought tonight.

She empties her fourth glass.

"You're pretty, Alice. I'm happy you're pretty at least." Her gaze attempts to focus on me.

Alixx glances slowly from Konstance to me and then back again. With his wings, he looks like the devil plotting his sin. Nothing good can come from Alixx paying too close attention. He seems to have a thing for exploiting people's weaknesses, and I know he's picking apart every single word I say or don't say.

My lips part, and before I can think of a petty half compliment to match hers, she carries on without me. "I'd absolutely die if my brother's wife gave us ugly babies to inherit our Wanderlust throne."

My eyebrows lift, and I decide just to take a long drink of my water instead.

"Sorry," Constantine whispers under his breath to me. His gaze doesn't linger on mine before he smiles up at his belligerently drunk sister.

"Constantine wants me to bond with you, share secrets, and become the best of friends." The tense smile Konstance gives me is uncomfortable to look at. "I'll start, I suppose." She thinks for the smallest moment. "Is it hard for you?" she asks very suddenly and, despite my mouth opening, she doesn't wait for any words to come out. "I find it impossible to orgasm, and other women tell me the female climax isn't a myth, but it—it's hard, right? I just get so anxious about it, and the nicknames don't help. They give me these awful nicknames that just make me so damn self-conscious. How can any woman bring herself to orgasm when they call you Snarl Snatch?"

My eyes widen at that. Constantine shakes his head at her, attempting to get her to stop rambling with a silent plea while Alixx stifles his laughter, coughing here and there before clearing his throat several times but chuckling throughout.

"If you'll excuse me, my darling." Alixx nods to his betrothed. He stands, making him seem even taller as he stares down at us all. "I think I'll grab us another bottle of Rosen and really loosen you out of your shell." He places his fingers obnoxiously close to hers, his little finger twitching just slightly, threatening to touch her with the smallest fraction of skin against skin.

She topples out of her chair to get away, her layered gown fluffing up around her as she lands in the damp grass on her ass, struggling to sit up to a kneeling position.

"My sweet beloved," Alixx hisses a bit dramatically and, with a slicing smile, his voice drops so low I barely hear him. "I never expected to see you on your knees again, sweetheart."

"Be careful, Rotter." The King's sister glares daggers at the man, and Constantine quickly rounds the table to help her stand while she continues to look at Alixx through hateful steely eyes. "Maybe it'd be better if you left. It's getting late," she snaps out.

Oh no.

"That's not necessary, Konstance," her brother whispers, chancing a glance over his shoulder to remind himself that I'm still here.

Still here. Unfortunately.

"I'm going to use the restroom really quick." I stand slowly, and Konstance shifts her glaring eyes from Alixx to me which is more than I can say for her brother, because he doesn't acknowledge me at all.

I exhale slowly before trailing through the rose garden. My fingers skim along the white petals, and glitter shines against my fingertips as I go. Everything here is beautiful. Beautiful on the surface and dangerous underneath, it seems.

The ground is soft, and I sink with each step I take, my heels lowering down into the dirt, letting the hem of my new white dress drag along the grass. I can't find it in me to care. I hope the whole damn dress gets wet and muddy from neckline to hem.

None of it matters. Does this charade, this Alice Game,

does it matter?

What am I really signing up for here? I thought I was getting a fairy tale life. A life I should have had. It seems I'm getting a loveless life, and that hurts to think about. I'm not overly romantic, but I did think the guy I married would be attracted to me. What kind of fucked up life am I creating when I'm clearly more attracted to my demented future brother-in-law than I am my future husband?

An awkward one. Definitely an awkward life.

My heels click when they meet brick, and I trail toward the back doors. They split down the middle, creating large French doors that lead into an empty sitting room. Kais said I could take a left and it'd lead down a long corridor. I scurry down the dark hall. The estate is quiet, but I do hear murmurs when I pass what appears to be the kitchen door. I hurry past it before someone can spot the wandering girl who's about to commit treason because a white rabbit said it'd be a good idea.

Someone reserve me a room at the nearest mental institute; I've clearly gone mad.

The sex dungeon is just around this corner. I turn to the right just as Kais described.

And come face to face with pale white features looming in the darkness.

The scream that slips from my lips is covered quickly by my hand. We stand in the dark, the prophet and I, both trying to figure out why the other is here. The young boy is blocking the door to the lower level.

"Hi," I say, smoothing my gown.

"Hello, Madison." His head tilts, but he doesn't say more. An odd feeling slips down my spine when his gaze lowers to my bare shoulders and the top of my dress that's tight against my breasts.

The small amount of moonlight illuminates his pale features, pale hair and stark black clothes. I hate how creeped out the small boy makes me. I shouldn't feel this uneasy around a child, should I?

"I was…just looking for the restroom."

Shit, can he tell if I'm lying?

"Your mother says she's not angry."

My stomach twists hard, attempting to shelter itself from the eerie words the boy just spoke.

"I'm sorry, what?"

"Your mom. She's not angry you missed her funeral."

I back away from him, my heart and my stomach both squeezing painfully.

"Listen, *Sixth Sense*, if you could just point me in the direction of a restroom." My gaze never once lifts to the door behind him, and I try my best to block out the things he just said about my mom.

"I would, but you owe me."

He seems old and young all at the same time. His stance is that of an arrogant man who's somehow earned the right to be cocky and condescending. It's the strangest sight to see in a little boy.

"I owe you?" My arms fold, and neither of us moves an inch.

"I gave you a message. Messages from beyond aren't as pricey as messages from the future. Messages from the past that you've overlooked—those are the cheapest, but all of them come at a price."

This is what Kais was trying to tell me all along. Not Prophet. *Profit.*

Clever boy.

Nothing in this life is free.

Except that message he just delivered. Because I'm a broke college student whose debt will likely loom over me into every realm I fall into.

Including this one.

"I think I'll have to owe you. I didn't bring my wallet"—into this realm—"with me tonight."

"It's not a pay as you go situation, bitch." His eyes harden, looking years older than just a twelve-year-old boy once again.

A light crackling hisses through the room.

"Hey, save your pet names for your King, Preston." Alixx slips in at my side from literally thin air, scaring the shit out of me even more.

I take a small breath and realize what Alixx said at the end. "Preston? Aw, that's cute."

Preston's eyes roll, and he glares over at Alixx whose chest almost brushes my arm. "It's Profit, and the bitch owes me."

"Call her a bitch again and you'll have to find someone to deliver your messages while *you're* in the afterlife, Preston." Alixx unfolds two bills, and the boy is careful not to touch the man's hand when he rips the money from him.

And then he runs off, turning the corner so fast, his sneakers squeak.

"Sorry." I keep my arms folded, my attention slipping over toward the curved torture dungeon door.

"Everyone gets conned by the Profit a time or two. He'll try it again on you. Don't let your guard down."

My gaze slips toward the man still lingering close to my side, almost touching but not quite.

"Is he real though? What he tells people, the messages he delivers, do you think he's real?" I swallow hard as I think about what he said about my mom.

Alixx nods slowly. "I think so. Preston's mother is said to have been a real life medium. One of the best."

"Wow. That's amazing."

"Yeah, she used him as a conduit a lot. A host of sorts. Real nice fucking woman."

A conduit…the word doesn't ring a bell, but the idea of that little boy being a host of some kind for spirits paints an alarming picture.

A chill slithers down my spine. I can see how stiff and defensive his shoulders are held. I don't know what connection Alixx has to Preston, but he seems to hate Preston's mother. Hell, after hearing that little fact, I hate Preston's mom now too, but it seems deeper for Alixx. Something I can't explain.

"You hate his mom?"

He looks at me from under his thick dark lashes. "I hate mothers who use their children in the worst possible way. So, yeah, I hate Preston's mom."

Just mothers? Maybe it isn't Preston's mom at all. Maybe it's Alixx's mother who's giving him this foreign rage that I've never seen in him before.

"If you're headed to the lower level, we need to go now. The King asked me to check on you before I leave for the night," Alixx says with a long sigh that seems to pull the tension right out of his shoulders.

"What makes you think I'm going to the dungeon?"

Alixx's lips tilt at one side with a curving half-smile.

"Because Kais isn't as smart as he thinks he is. Anyone with a bit of time to kill would be able to tell that the King's most

trusted advisor is a fucking traitor."

My eyes snap wide open.

"Shut up," I hiss, covering his mouth with my hand. With little strength, he seems to let me control his body with a light shove. His back hits the wall. He stiffens against my touch, my chest pressed to his. But he never touches me. His hands stay carefully positioned at his sides. "Do not ever suggest that again. Don't even think it. Don't connect treason to Kais, and do not connect treason to me. Understand?"

From above my fingers, his green eyes glint in the moonlight shining in from the small window. It's that amused watchful look he gets when he dissects people slowly. Seconds pass. He never nods. His teeth bare, and he bites me just hard enough to sting pain into my palm.

I jerk back from him in an instant. "You fucking bit me."

"You fucking offered your hand up to be bitten." He takes a step closer, another and another until I'm forced to back up from his continued steps. The emptiness in his expression is an ominous sight, and I'm suddenly second-guessing what I thought I knew about Alixx Stone. "Don't threaten me again, Madison. I like you. I really do. But the next time your hands press to my body, I won't stop at just a playful bite or a deliciously chaste kiss. I'm not a playful man." The sinister smile that pulls across his lips makes energy pool in my chest. Some of it's fear…and some of it's unexplainable desire.

What in the twisted fuck is wrong with me? This guy's screwed up in the head from too many years of isolation, and instead of running from his threats, I'm considering slipping my tongue against his just to taste the nasty words he constantly spews to everyone.

He pauses for a single moment with a real look of concern flashing in his features. "Don't believe everything Kais pretends to be either." He speaks carefully. Not hesitantly but precisely. "He's not as innocent as his controlled exterior seems. He's a dangerous man, Alice."

After all my threats, I'm not sure what to say to that. I don't know who to trust and who to believe in this place.

Maybe I shouldn't trust any of them.

Seconds pass during the few moments we test one another with our glaring gazes. His wings ruffle quietly, straightening themselves before pulling in tight against his back. His hand lifts, and he pulls the door open with a quiet screech of the hinges.

"After you, sweet Alice." He gestures toward the open door, his chest still pressing to mine, his gaze searching very carefully over my face.

I side step out of his space, keeping my gaze locked with his until I slowly descend the stone stairs to the prison dungeon. Darkness wraps around me, making my echoed footsteps seem more pronounced the farther and farther I stumble down.

Fire erupts in blooming brightness on the side of the wall. It flashes so fast it hurts my eyes at first to see it. Torches light of their own accord, one after the other along the wall. The light chases down into the darkness. I turn back to see Alixx pulling his hand away from the first fiery flame. He gives another of his easy manic smiles, pushing his chest against my shoulder as he passes, and leads the way down the long brick staircase. For several minutes, all that can be heard is Alixx's even steps and the hesitant clicking of my heels following after him.

It feels odd to be trailing down after a psychopath to the dungeon of doom. My recent decisions in life have become even more questionable at best. I'm so focused on the uneven concrete steps, carefully placing my foot on each jagged brick, that I don't notice when Alixx turns abruptly, stopping dead in his tracks.

Worst of all, he notices me not noticing. He's ready. Liter-

ally welcoming me with open arms.

My face smooshes unattractively into something smooth yet hard. My fingers splay across said hard surface, spreading wide against soft cotton over perfectly chiseled abs just as his big hands slip low on my back, holding me to him in the most ridiculously romantic embrace.

That raspy breathy tone of his fans across my neck and ear in a way he seems to enjoy doing, sending tingling goosebumps all across my skin. "If you wanted to get me alone, all you had to do was say so, my sweet Alice."

I shove off of him hard, making me stumble back until my ass hits the bottom step.

I suddenly feel very much like Konstance: thrown down on the floor simply because I can't stand to touch him. Will he ridicule me the way he ridiculed her?

Tension in my chest presses to get out as I stare up at the careless man to see if I'm another mockery in his life.

That fucking smile stays pulled across his sneering lips while he looks down on me poised at his feet. Seconds slip by between us, covered in our strangled silence.

And then he lowers his hand to me. Without a word, he offers me the smallest minuscule of kindness that I didn't even know he was capable of.

My fingers slip into his rough palm, the warmth of his touch is firm against my hand as he heaves me up, pulling me right back up to the place I pushed so hard to get away from. He keeps my hand in his while his eyes shine like flames in the firelight.

"Come along, sweet Alice," is all he says just before he releases me and leads the way into the large open dungeon.

Warm golden color blooms out from the center of the room. It flickers and dances with each candle that burns from the shining chandelier above. A small romantic dinner table sits in the center of the room. It's prepared for two, and each chair is set with a large cup of wafting hot tea. One more lone candle stick is there on the small table, and I have to admit, for a torture dungeon, this place has some serious mood lighting.

"Hello, Alice."

Every muscle in my body tenses from the mysterious voice. My eyes dart around the shadows of the brick room. Not a single person can be seen.

Alixx pulls out a chair, letting it scrape harshly against the dark brick before he plops down and kicks his feet up hard enough to shake the table and slop the tea over the brim of the cups. His wings spread out wider around the chair in the most casual way. He lounges there with his hands held arrogantly behind his dark hair, getting comfortable like he knows he'll be here for a while.

"Over here, girl."

My eyes widen when I stare at where the voice is coming from. A solid wooden door, curved at the top with gleaming metallic embellishments is there.

No one else.

The silver infinity symbol in the center of the wood narrows, glaring at me, and the wood above the symbol furrows like a low brow. My heart hammers while I stare at it, but I can't get a word to force up my throat.

The silver knocker thins together, pursing tightly while that peculiar infinity symbol continues to glare hard at me.

"Well, I haven't got all night," the knocker says, my shoulders stiffening harder with every word the metallic mouth says. "Either drink the tea or don't, but don't stand there gawking. It's rude."

"For once, I'm not the rude one." Alixx looks back at me

with his half-smile in place. "Morrison, this is Madison. Madison, may I present, Morrison, the door."

The way he says my name pulls at my attention, but the oddness of the situation demands all of my attention. I blink at Morrison. I blink for so long the door sighs at my stupidity.

"Well?" Morrison the door eyes me, making me shift on my feet from the bizarrely human way his metal symbols moves.

"You're a door, and your name's Morrison?" I arch an eyebrow and wonder if the door himself realizes he's been named after a rock star.

"She's not the brightest I've ever met," Morrison mutters.

Nope. He doesn't realize it. Shame.

I shuffle a little closer, letting my heels click slowly against the brick.

"Can I get through here?" I point to him, and the door levels me with a bored expression.

"There's a toll fee, of course." Morrison arches that metal brow at me.

A toll fee. I'm finding there are a lot of toll fees in Wanderlust.

"Take a seat, drink some tea," the door says.

I pull out the chair across from Alixx and lower myself slowly into it. The metal wiring backrest gives me the most proper posture.

"So I'll drink the tea, and then I'll be small enough to crawl through your key hole?" I lift a confused hand at all of this, trying to remember what it was that Alice did to get through the Wonderland door.

"I beg your pardon?" Morrison gives a disgusted, unhinged look. That's right, a door is giving an *unhinged* look. What the fuck is going on with my life? "Who is this girl you brought

151

me, Rotter? Never in all my years has a woman had the nerve to suggest she go mucking around in my hole."

"You know, she suggested the same thing to me when we first met. I couldn't turn her down though," Alixx whispers to the door, adding a hinting wink in the most obnoxious way.

Oh my God. He's the worst. The absolute worst person I could have brought to help me in all of this. I glare across the romantic table at my date, and he has the fucking audacity to smirk at me. Okay, so the sexy, obnoxious smirk was already there; it never really left, but fuck him for turning it my way.

"That's not—never mind. What do I do with the tea?"

Morrison takes a bit longer to finally address me, "Drink the Sinceri Tea, and then we'll carry on with the next step."

"What's the next step?"

Alixx's amusement slips, growing serious with concern as he listens closely, and the somber look on his face only puts me that much more on edge.

"We will get to the next step once you complete the first step." Morrison's tone never wavers, he doesn't press, and he and I both know I'm not in the position to fight him.

My hands clasp over the large white cup. The words *Drink Me* are scrawled in delicate letters across the front. The warmth of the steam hits my lips just before I press the large mug to my mouth. My eyes lift, meeting Alixx's stern gaze as the tea meets my tongue. I focus on him as I drink every last drop down. I thought it would comfort me to remind myself that I'm not alone right now, to keep my attention on him instead of the nervousness that's crawling up my stomach.

But the uneasy look in his eyes isn't comforting at all.

I feel it the moment the Sinceri Tea takes effect. Everything feels slower. The way my eyes blink, the turn of my head,

even the breaths I take feel slow and delayed. It's like I barely even need air to survive right now.

"Time for step two." Morrison's metal mouth curves into the smallest smile. "Sinceri Tea forces honesty. The Wanderlust that I'm crafted from reacts to secrets. I'm a door starved for secrets, Alice. Feed me your truths, and see if they're enough to gain you entrance to what lies on the other side."

Secrets. Shit.

I stand, my feet moving as if they're lodged in thick mud. I take the few steps toward Morrison. His door handle shines against the candle light. I don't want whatever wonders are on the other side. I just need to pull a lever for wanderfuck's sake.

My secrets are mine. They're the things I wanted to keep in my old life. Not the things I wanted to drag with me into my new life.

I won't give them up. Especially not in front of someone as malicious as Alixx Stone.

With as much speed as my sluggish mind can manage, I grip his handle and turn, attempting to force the thing to open.

A horrified shriek leaves the knocker's mouth, his knob wiggles under my touch, not turning in the least. There's a moment of struggle, my hand twisting, his knob jerking. A big hand claps around my hips and pulls me away from the door. I reluctantly release it.

"How dare you!" Morrison bellows.

Alixx keeps me in place, holding me back from the anger in Morrison's silver eyes.

"You just go around grabbing knobs now, do you?" Morrison shakes his silver door handle as if he's adjusting himself, and it hits me hard what he associates his knob with. Vomit stings the back of my throat as he continues to shake it once, twice, yep, three times. My lips part, but not one word gurgles from my mortified mouth.

I swear my right hand has never felt so damn dirty in its entire life.

"I'm so, *so* sorry, Morrison. I didn't realize…" I continue to hold my hands awkwardly up in front of myself so his dick-knob germs don't touch anything. I can't think clearly enough to say any more.

Morrison gives another stiff shake of his handle, his thin lips finally parting to speak to me again.

"Secrets. Let's get this unfortunate meeting over with."

I nod, and I don't shove out of Alixx's hold on me this time. His hands against my hips, his chest pressing to my back feel strong and grounding as my stomach knots nervously around itself. If I don't look at him, if I don't meet his watchful eyes, I might be able to say all the things I never wanted anyone else to hear about me.

It's a terrible feeling to think about the things you try to hide from everyone. It's unexplainably worse when you go to confess those things.

"Just start small," Alixx whispers against my hair.

I nod, swallowing down the thick nervousness that's filling my throat.

"I'm a virgin." I lick my lips and see if that little confession unlocks and sends Morrison wide open.

It. Does. Not.

"It's not really a secret if it's something even The Rotter knows, girl."

I can almost feel the smug smile pulling against Alixx's lips.

"Right." I blink a few times, stalling and thinking through

the weakest secrets I own. "I-I hated my life before I came here."

"Now we're getting somewhere," Morrison says in a humming voice.

It's weird but, once a few little secrets slip out, the rest start to push and shove to climb up my throat. That's the tea kicking in, I guess.

"I missed my mother's funeral, and I'll never admit how a part of me was relieved because I didn't want the image of her in a casket to taint my memories of her just as she was." I close my eyes and keep them closed, letting a long breath exit my lungs, taking a small amount of building ache with it.

Alixx pulls me closer to him, holding me harder to his body until the nervousness in me is replaced by the sudden realization that I like the feel of his body against mine.

More words press painfully against my chest, demanding to come out. I take a smaller intake of air, my hands lowering, shaking slightly before gripping Alixx's with more force than I realize. His fingers intertwine through mine in the most soothing way.

And then I say the one thing I never wanted anyone here to know.

"I was diagnosed with leukemia a month before I came here. A reoccurrence. I was ready to give up. I was miserable. I was tired of being tired." At the quiet sound of my words, strong arms wrap fully around me, hugging me and holding me and making me believe they'll never let me go. "Wanderlust cured me. This world gave me a second chance—it gave me a first chance. A first real chance at a real life. At happiness. And I'll pretend to be whatever they want me to be as long as they let me stay." My breath catches, shuddering out in the weakest gasp.

I'm terrified that Alixx will use what I just said against me in some way. But for now, I'll let myself pretend he's every bit the friend he appears to be in this moment.

Hinges crawl on a squeaking sound, drawing that sound out until it echoes around the dimly lit room.

"You did it," Alixx whispers.

My lashes lift to find the big wooden door open. Morrison's face is to the wall, and he doesn't say another word while I stare up at what lies beyond.

A blue and white surface ripples before me. It appears as if a layer of water veils the entryway. It looks like a portal of some kind. Beautiful and mysterious.

"What's on the other side?" I can't steady my voice no matter how hard I try.

"I have no fucking idea." The low tone of Alixx's words is gentle but doesn't relax me at all. What he says next doesn't help either. "No one comes down here. The few people who have, never came back."

Fear drills into me with the hard pounding of my heart.

Alixx knows everything about everyone. It's terrifying to think he doesn't know what's beyond this door.

I blink hard, trying to clear my mind from the Sinceri Tea. This is all such a terrible fucking idea. Why would they drug you and throw you into something that's clearly dangerous?

I force an even breath from my lungs, pleading with my own senses to calm and return to a cognitive state as if I can simply demand it.

I open my eyes as far as they'll go. Close them. Squint a little. Open them again.

I'm a stupid drunk. I'm "that girl," apparently. That one who fakes alertness by simply widening her eyes to a raccoon state.

Fuck my life right now.

I take a timid step forward, and the strong arms wrapped around my stomach loosen but don't fall away.

He's still holding me.

I turn, stumbling just slightly, and he keeps his palms low on my back like it's the most natural thing in the world.

I won't admit how much I like it.

"This might be goodbye, sweet Alice." His lips pull up at the corner, but the smile doesn't feel as easy and genuine as it normally does. It's tinged with just a bit of sadness that hurts my chest deep at the center.

In the time that I've been here, I've heard a few things about *The Rotter*. They say he's deadly. A killer. An assassin.

I don't know if I believe that. When I look into the depths of his eyes, I don't see something evil.

When he's not making me crazy, I see something good within all the bad that is Alixx Stone.

After tonight, he's only made me believe that even more.

He's been so patient during all of this.

Such an ally. Such a friend.

"If you want me to take your virtue, now's the time to ask." At that, the sneer does curve his lips fully.

Such an asshole.

Even when I think that he might not be, he still fucking is.

I push his arms down, stepping fully out of his disgustingly sweet embrace.

"I think I'll pass. No need to be completely disappointed just before I die."

His palm presses to his heart like I just fatally wounded him.

I turn, taking another step closer to that rippling, illuminating veil. Mere inches separate me from whatever is on the other side.

I could leap. Right now. Throw logic aside and leap into what I have to do.

A deep breath hits my lungs. My body tenses. I'm ready.

Right. Now.

A hand pulls at mine, breaking down every ounce of confidence I'd just built up.

My teeth clench together, and I meet those deep green eyes. The nasty glint of amusement that always shines in his gaze isn't there.

"Why'd you kiss me, Madison?" His big hand lingers in mine. The sincerest look of curiosity is in his striking features.

And for the second time since I've been here, someone's asking me why I kissed Alixx Stone, The Rotter, Outcast, and Assassin Extraordinaire.

"I'm about to leap to my death right now, but you'd like me to pause to stroke your ego?" My lip tilts at the corner, and his mouth twitches until he's biting back a smile as well.

"I mean, it couldn't hurt. Spare just a few seconds for my poor lack of confidence, please." His thumb brushes back and forth against my knuckles, his gaze holding hard on mine. So hard that I think he might kiss me all over again.

But he doesn't. No matter how many little touches he passes me, how many curious glances he trails over my body, he won't cross that line.

Not with me.

I kissed him to remind him he was still alive. He's alive and he has a life worth living. If he can just ignore all the whispers society says about him.

We're alike in that way.

"I kissed you for the same reason you constantly run your hands over my body at every chance you get. I kissed you just be-

cause I knew that I could." His brow lowers, and maybe he doesn't understand right now, but I know he'll dissect every single word until it all makes sense.

I just won't be here when it does.

My hand slips from his, and I memorize his startlingly handsome features as I fall back, letting my weight pull me down into the unknown. Cold liquid sloshes over me, hitting my face first and enveloping me like greedy hands pulling me under.

My eyes clench closed, my body stiffening hard.

It's the most peculiar feeling of being present but also being washed away. Dissolved down until every fiber of your being feels like nothingness. It's the strangest, most terrible feeling.

Being here one minute and gone the next.

Chapter Twenty-One

Madison

I wish I could say the graceful way I'd fallen backward was how I stayed when I found myself deep in the unknown.

It was not.

My hands flail through the cold water, tangling myself up in the beautiful layers of my dress like a sheet set out to dry in a fucking windstorm. At some point, my blonde hair wafts over my gaping mouth, and I flail around a little more, using my dress-tangled hands to push it all away like messy hair might be the absolute worst thing that could happen to me right now.

I float, feeling weighted but also weightless as I descend down into the depths of the mysterious water. My eyes open slowly. It's the clearest water. Rays of bright, unobtainable light shine down on me from somewhere high overhead. It casts the smooth white sand, the jagged beautiful coral and the few scurrying black and yellow fish into abnormally bright colors.

It's all familiar but…not.

It must be the ocean. It has to be. But it's an unrealistically perfect vision of the sea. I can't see the shining ripples of the surface. I'm so far down I can feel the press of the water. And yet, every detail is in crisp color.

Including the long, thick blue tentacle curling around a very shining lever on the ocean floor. The metallic handle is so out of place, so man-made here among the soft feel of nature. The giant tentacle coiled around the base of it doesn't look out of place though. That tree trunk of a blue limb looks like it's been poised leisurely there for centuries.

Waiting.

Kais gave me very precise directions on how to get to the lever.

He seems to have forgotten some minor details about what happens after getting through the dungeon door.

The body of the monstrous creature is unseen. The long and winding path of its limb leads to a patch of coral and slate gray rocks. Somewhere behind that mound is an angry octopus who's missing a limb thanks to me.

I untangle my dress, but it just wafts around me all over again, revealing my legs and reminding me to kick off the useless heels. My lungs ache for air, but it isn't an urgent thought in my mind. With slow movements, I kick steady, careful inches closer to the beast I know I should fear. The dress is impossible to swim in, but I'm not exactly racing around doing laps either. I take small, quiet, and meager little strokes toward the lever.

My fist bunches into my gown, forcing it not to touch the tentacle. Keeping myself afloat above the lever while also trying to figure out how to pull it without the creature knowing is an awful situation. I fumble around for a few seconds, pulling and tugging and ultimately getting nowhere.

It's not just an awful situation. It's an impossible task.

Another pain presses in my chest, my lungs begging for air.

There's no visible way out of this.

The lever is right here.

I have to do what I set out to do.

My foot balances onto the soft silt, gently settling down between the loosely coiled tentacle. The long limb looks like a noose from where I stand looking down on it. My ankle is in the snare, seeming just mere inches from being captured.

I swallow painfully and keep my other leg held up in a sort of flamingo-like stance while I cling to the lever. What will happen when I pull it, surely jostling the creature who's clinging to the base of this thing?

I guess I'm going to find out.

Without a breath in my burning lungs and with the thudding of my heart beating in my ears, I put all my weight into pulling back the handle. It moves the slightest little bit. I feel the iron grinding, and the smallest tilt of the lever encourages me on with so much urgency I slam my other foot down, letting my ankle roll against the curve of the slick limb beneath it.

Movement slides between my calves. Sand shakes up from the ground, lifting with so much power that it clouds my sight. Harder I pull, needing to finish this now. Right now.

It doesn't budge. The metal bites into my palms, but I grip it with both hands and use the big tentacle beneath my bare feet as leverage as I heave back with all my shaking might.

Tightness strangles around my legs, bringing me down. Stinging pain sears into my skin, but still I cling to that lever. The billowing sand lifts higher around me, blocking out whatever creature is looming behind me, and that is the only upside to this fuck hole of a situation.

The long blue tentacle abandons the handle, focusing its painful strength solely on me. The air leaves my lungs in one big whoosh as the octopus wraps its grip fully around my torso.

One of my hands falls away while the other holds on like it's the only thing I have left keeping me here in this life.

And then the creature rips me away. The power it puts into tearing me away is exactly what I didn't realize I needed.

The lever follows me down, flipping all the way down with me just before my hand slips off of it. The octopus did all the heavy lifting for me.

And now I'm going to meet my fate.

Tighter he holds me, crushing the life right out me in the slowest, most torturous way. Pain breaks harder into me, cracking through my body with each passing second.

Then the sand swirls around, twirling my long hair as my lashes start to flutter. The movement of the water is unnatural and demanding.

That's what seems to set him off.

The creature stiffens. Then its hold on me loosens little by little until it pulls away in one quick jerk. It leaves faster than I can follow. My body falls, drifting down at a leisurely pace just before my face settles against the soft sand. My eyelids blink, heavy and tired, seeing the world in a blur of bright beautiful colors.

There in front of me is…a drain.

Sand funnels through it, circling it at a rather rapid speed.

A shadow bleeds across the white sand. It's an ominous, terrifying thing that blocks out the light above. But I don't have the strength to move. My fingers twitch against my palm, urging me to find a motive to swim, to scurry away like the rest of the wildlife here seems to be doing as they pass my limp body by.

My foot shoves against the base of the lever, and pain

shoots through my leg, but I try to push away from the shadow that's growing closer by the minute. My dress pulls against my body, caught on something, and I don't move a single inch.

I wait with my lashes slipping closed, my drilling heartbeat slowing strangely.

Warm hands press to my hips, alarming my heart rate once again, reminding me that fear is very much still alive within me. He turns me, and my lashes flutter open. Calm spreads through me when I look up into Alixx's emerald eyes. He pulls me up against him but doesn't lift me far. My dress tangles around my legs, not giving me any room to move as it strains, caught on something. My attention drifts slowly down, finding the hem of my white dress bunched into the base of the lever, jammed there, keeping me in place.

Alixx pulls hard at the material. The muscles of his biceps flex, but the white fabric doesn't tear away.

My lashes flutter once more, almost closing entirely.

He holds me tightly to his chest, meeting my gaze and making me wonder if I'll die here on the bottom of the ocean with this beautifully tormented man holding me in his arms.

Warm fingers trail down my spine, but I feel his touch in every part of my body. The gentle delicious feel of his hands drives out all the pain for just a moment.

The last thing I remember is Alixx Stone's fingers searing across every inch of my skin: my ribs, my stomach, hips, and thighs.

If this is death, maybe I've never really lived.

Chapter Twenty-Two

Kais

The fucker's looking at me like he's won some sort of prize instead of nearly killing the one woman who can fix the world we live in.

The sickly fond way he holds her against his chest shoots more anger into me. He cradles her in his arms like she's something he cherishes. I'm careful not to touch him as I pull her nearly naked body away from his disturbing affection. She doesn't wake.

But she is breathing.

And then I see it. From the chest down, every inch of her body is purple and black, bruising deep into her ivory skin.

"What the fuck did you do to her?"

"Just took her out. Showed her a good time. The usual," he says dismissively, crossing one ankle casually over the other as he leans against the side of my house. His dark hair hangs wet and messy across his temple.

"You touched her. You held her with your bare hands, you fucking lunatic." I can't stand the thought of releasing her, letting her fragile body go just to save myself from whatever Rotter-ish plague he's given her.

I'll kill him for hurting her.

"Unfortunately, that's not my branding. I didn't hurt her. *You,* you fucking hurt her." He points his finger at me, cocking his head while he continues lounging lazily against my house. "You sent her through a portal when you didn't even know what was on the other side. So, here's a thought: The next time you want your dirty work done, do it yourself like a fucking gentleman, Rabbit." He adjusts his sopping wet tie like he's the classiest man who ever donned a goddamn saturated suit.

I pause, holding her cold body to my chest, letting her drench the front of my white t-shirt with her long blonde hair. She nuzzles her face into the crook of my neck, and the energy that shoots straight down to my cock isn't helping our situation.

A knowing smirk slashes across Rotter's lips. "I should leave. It looks like you have your hands full." His gaze trails down, noting how close my actual hand is to the curve of her ass.

He brings her back, lifeless in just her bra and panties, and then walks away without an explanation. My teeth grit together hard, distracting the tingling sensation this woman is pressing into my body. Just before I speak, he cuts me off.

"I'm not a rebel, Kais. I get paid a good salary. I live a… mundane life. I like it that way," he says as he strolls away with his hands in his pockets. He pauses to make good condescending eye contact. "Don't put me in the middle of your traitor games again. And if you weren't such a selfish fuck, you wouldn't put this girl in the middle either."

Rotter turns on the heels of his shining black shoes, but as much as I hate speaking to him, one question must be asked.

"Did the King see her?" The words are quiet, but he stiffens, stopping in his tracks the moment I say them.

"No. I guarded the door. I waited. I waited some more. And then I saved your little pet's life. Vanished her right out of the dungeon. I'd suggest, if you are not accepting New Fake Alices, you take better care of the one you've got, Traitor."

He strides away, and I know the only reason he doesn't vanish himself right now is because he wants the pleasure of making a dramatic fucking exit.

I roll my eyes, hating how much he gets under my skin and hating how fucking right he is.

Unlike Rotter, I do vanish us. I sweep Madison and me away until I'm standing at my bed, cradling her in my arms and counting her warm breaths that fan against my neck.

She's okay.

She's soft, fragile, and bruised.

But she's okay.

I lie her down against the old blanket and immediately take off my shirt. I pull it over her head, it's large around her shoulders. There's a tear at the hem, but it falls down across her silk bra and panties. It covers her for the most part. A cold chill shakes through her body. The shirt isn't enough. The smooth length of her long legs trembles against my touch as I maneuver her beneath the warm blanket. She curls in on herself.

Seeming content. Safe.

I can't believe I let this happen to her.

I have no idea what I sent her into. But I can see now, she's just as strong as she pretends to be. Resilient and determined.

If I didn't know any better, I'd think she really was the savior Profit spoke of all those years ago.

"Kais?" Her lips barely move to speak my name, and I'm

on my knees in front of her in an instant.

She brings me to my knees that fast.

I growl orders at her all day, and she fights me every step of the way, but the weakness I feel right now for her is insane. It should be setting off alarm bells of all kinds in my mind.

But all I can focus on is her needs. Whatever she wants, I'll do it. I'm the reason she's hurt. This is my fault.

"What is it?" I whisper.

"I did it. I followed orders. For once." A smile attempts to reach her lips just as her lashes lower, flittering to try to stay open.

Her words stab guilt right into me. She *followed orders*. Fuck. For once, I wish she hadn't. Not like this.

"Yeah. You did it perfectly." I try to be proud of her, but I hate myself right now.

My hand lifts, but I lower it just as quickly, forcing myself to keep my hands to myself.

Her lashes rise, pinning those pale green eyes on me, sending too many feelings darting through my chest with a single fucking look of her beautiful gaze.

"It was terrible, Kais." Unbearable guilt tangles through my stomach harder at the sound of her whispered words. "Every time I close my eyes, I feel it all over again."

Fuck, Rotter was more than right. I am a selfish fuck for using her.

My palm lifts once again, and I carefully cradle her jaw, letting my fingers thread through her hair, pushing it back from her sweet face.

"I'm sorry, Madison." My tone is too gruff, raw, a little painful.

Her hand moves slowly, and I watch it even as she slides

her fingers along mine against the side of her face.

She doesn't acknowledge my apology, and I know it's just one of many I'll say to her.

She says something else entirely instead.

"Sleep with me," she whispers.

Tension strikes right through me. My lips part, but she speaks again.

"Make me feel safe. Make me feel—" Whatever else she doesn't say is quietly cut off, and I find myself hanging on what she doesn't say.

What does she want me to make her feel? My blood pulses through my body with the idea of all the dirty things I'll never make her feel.

I lick my lips slowly, and before my brain can talk my dick out of it, I'm slipping beneath her covers.

Stiffly, I lie flat on my back, keeping a precarious inch of space between her soft curves and my body.

But it doesn't last.

A long leg slides over my thigh, slipping between my legs, her core melding to my side just as her head settles against my shoulder. She wraps herself around me like I'm unsuspecting prey. All of my defensive military training goes out the window all because a pretty girl used her body like a weapon.

If the King acts as fucking stupid as I am right now, he won't stand a chance against Madison.

Long fingers skim over my bare chest, demanding my heart to beat harder just for her. Quiet, even breaths tickle over my skin, and I gently push my palm to a platonic place along her knee.

She's at peace. I've made her feel safe just like she asked.

Even if I won't get a single second of sleep tonight with

her pussy pressed hard against me.

It's early when I wake. I wake to the amazing feeling of soft hands trailing over every inch of my chest. A low groan hums through me just before I open my eyes to the dark wooden ceiling. For several seconds, I just lie there. As still as possible while her fingertips trace delicate, tormenting lines over my skin. It takes me a second to realize she's tracing my tattoos, following the path they carve down my chest, my stomach, my hips. When my dick hardens against her inner thigh, her fingers stop abruptly.

My palm rose sometime in the middle of the night. That platonic place I left it before I fell asleep is not that platonic place I find it when I wake.

My fingers flex ever so subtly along the curve of her ass and the back of her thigh.

I should move my hand.

I should.

I'm not a fucking idiot.

I'm just—I'm the worst fucking human being that ever stepped foot into this beautiful realm. I'm a traitor. I am. I can pretend to be the good guy all I want, but I'll always make reckless decisions that don't quite follow the rules.

Like I am right now.

My palm slides slowly down the back of her thigh before trailing just as slowly right back up. My cock hardens even more when she instinctively rocks her hips against my side, rubbing her thigh against my cock in the best and worst way possible.

I'm going to fuck this all up.

I spent every night two feet away from this bed and her. Slept like shit every single night in that chair just to make sure there was a very defined line between her and me.

And now I'm here. Striking out that line and rewriting the goddamn definition of platonic. My self-control is thread thin, and now it's all unraveling right before my eyes.

Her head lifts, and I'm drawn to follow her. My head tilts down to hers. I find my fingers threaded into her thick red hair. Big green eyes look up at me, holding my gaze as her fingers start skimming down the lines of my abdomen all over again.

We give each other hesitant, consuming touches without ever saying a word. Because if we speak, I'll piss her off, and she'll make me crazy, and all of this will be ruined.

So we never say a word. But our bodies connect in a way words would never allow.

My palm slides back up the length of her leg, my thumb skimming back and forth along the line of her silk underwear. Her lips part, half an inch from my own, but she never looks away from me. Back down my palm glides, taking in every inch of her creamy thigh before pushing back up to the heat of her pussy.

I'm not a good guy.

I'm not responsible. I'm not honest. And I'm clearly not fucking smart.

Because my fingertips dip, sliding beneath her panties with the smallest move. Heat flares to life in her pretty eyes, and my fingers part her wetness, slipping down her wetness for just the shortest amount of half of a second.

Until my least favorite fucking Rebel Heart speaks.

"My, my, how the turns have tabled. You could cut the tension in this room with a spork," Lighton theater whispers, his arm brushing against mine from where he lies on his side right fucking next to me like we've somehow coordinated the world's most awkward threesome.

I pull my hand back, disengaging entirely from Madison

as I push out of the bed, shoving Lighton to the floor in the process. The bastard casually lies there flat on his back with a smile. He pushes his hands behind his head and just gets comfortable on the floor.

What pisses me off most is knowing he can't vanish into places. Therefore, he's been here for a while. Watching.

Madison's chest rises and falls with heavy breaths that match my own. My dick's still rock hard in my jeans, and I can still feel how wet she was against my fingertips.

And all of that was ruined because Lighton has zero understanding of personal space. He's been here since the day he arrived in Wanderlust, and he honestly is making no sign of leaving.

It's like he can't stand to be alone.

And I should probably be thanking him in this moment.

Because I crossed a line.

"She needs her rest."

"I bet she does," Lighton says with a smirk.

I pull a shirt from my drawer and, as always, simply ignore my uninvited guest.

"I have to meet with the King, but try to rest." Madison nods quietly to me, and I stand at the stairs, feeling more awkward than I ever have in my entire fucking life.

My hand was against her pussy thirty seconds ago, and now I can't even manage to make direct eye contact.

Fuck.

I pass a single glare at Lighton. He waves happily, and I curse him the entire way to the castle.

I curse him as well as thank him.

Chapter Twenty-Three

Madison

There's an ache between my thighs like I never could have imagined. I'm a virgin, but I'm far from innocent. The moment I was told I was in remission, I wanted a normal life. A happy life. And yeah, I wanted a sex life.

I craved normal the way most people crave the extraordinary.

I was one awkward Lighton comment away from having my first real sexual experience. With a guy who actually wanted me *and,* more importantly, could find a vagina.

I could see it though. Kais can pretend to be my guide and advisor all he wants, but something in him cracked this morning. I could see the want in his eyes.

He's a good guy, sure. But he's also a rebel. There's a rebellious streak in him.

And I want it.

"I brought you something," Lighton tells me, inching closer to me as he settles in against the headboard.

Unless it's an orgasm, I don't want it.

It's a petty thought but an honest one.

He pulls a small container from his pocket. The silver lid shines in the sunlight, and I wince when he bumps his shoulder into my side, sending searing hot pain shooting through my ribs.

He's gentle when he turns to me, opening the little canister for me to see the thick salve inside.

"Rotter said you were hurt," he whispers.

I peel the hem of Kais's shirt up and reveal the rope-like bruises lining my abdomen. I'm more exposed to him than I've ever been in just my underwear and a t-shirt, but all he focuses on are the parts of me in pain. His eyes widen, trailing over each mark covering my skin.

"Shit." His longer fingers dip into the canister, and he lightly applies the ointment to the darkest bruises along my ribs, the cold metal of his bracelet skimming over his work just lightly. "Trilune is a wild healing plant. Like everything else here, it only grows in Wonderland."

"How'd you get it in Wanderlust?"

He pauses for a single second before continuing.

"I have a source." He glances at me out of the corner of his eyes but quickly brings the subject back to the medicine. "It's rare, but we don't need to use much. It heals at a rapid speed." His whole palm skims over my navel, rubbing slowly against my skin, along every bruise from my toes all the way back up to the now pale purple bruises along my stomach. "Your ribs will be the slowest to heal, I think."

"Were you really a doctor?" I ask on a quiet breath, his hand settling heavily on my abdomen. He leans closer until his

chest is against my shoulder, and very little space separates me from him right now.

So I see it when his amber eyes darken, lashes lowering to avoid my gaze.

"No. I worked security for a corporate bank actually. It wasn't as interesting as anything Cat or Brody said."

"That's a good job. Don't make it sound meaningless. I bet you were really sexy in uniform."

He cracks at that. A smile pulls at his lips, and it warms me the way he smiles so easily.

"How'd you end up here?" I tilt my head at him while he works.

The smile fades. He doesn't meet my eyes again, continuing to tend to all the little bruises that are healing right before my very eyes.

But all I can focus on is the pain in his gaze.

"Light?" My hand settles gently over the back of his knuckles.

"I've just—I stopped drinking a few days after we talked at the falls, and everything's just a little harder to process, I guess." He tries to pull back, but I keep his hand held in mine.

"You stopped drinking?"

Because of me? Because of what I said?

He nods quietly.

"Three years ago, I was in a car accident. The truck blew the light and just demolished my passenger side." There's a small pause that has me curling into him from the empty look in his eyes. "My nine-year-old sister was in that seat." My breath cuts off as pain presses in on my lungs, and I know he hasn't even said the worst part yet. "She lived. She's been in a coma for three fucking years." His arm slips over my stomach so that he's holding himself

175

above me in the most intimate way. My fingers slip through his hair, and I stroke through his locks, trying to comfort him even as his eyes get this faraway look in them.

The odd silver bracelet…is it hers?

"Alcohol was never a problem for me in the surface world. But it is what led me here. After I visited her on her birthday last year—with no improvement to her condition—I got black out drunk. And I woke up here. I'm here in a fairy tale land. And she's still there. Still the same. Because of me." He swallows hard, and I pull him down against my chest, holding him to me to comfort him as well as myself.

I know now why Lighton doesn't want to feel the life he's living. The life he's living is miserable, riddled with memories and guilt.

"I'm fine, Cupcake." He pulls back from me, not letting me hug him and hold him.

"You're not fine, Lighton. You're allowed to feel pain."

Anger like I've never seen before slips into his eyes.

"Yeah. I am. And I fucking hate it. I don't want to feel it. I don't want to feel…anything." A tremor cracks through his voice, and he almost pulls away from me entirely.

Until I lean up into him, never letting him go. A beat passes. He stiffens when his attention drifts down to study the small distance between our mouths. His hands settle right back in place on my hips, and I instinctively lower my hands to his shoulders.

"You don't want to feel *anything*?" I whisper, letting my words fan against his lips.

He blinks at me as if he doesn't really know how to honestly answer that. The hamster that's been vacationing away from the wheel in Lighton's head has now come home, and he's appar-

ently more careful with his words now that he's sober.

It makes him silent more than he used to be.

"If you feel nothing all the time, you miss out on the best things in life." My chin tilts up, and he doesn't even wait for me before pressing his lips deliberately over mine, kissing me so slowly it's like he's making up for all the numbness he's felt for the last twelve months.

Or maybe longer.

One of his hands sinks into the mattress while his other hand snakes around my waist, holding me against him until my thighs part and he settles his hips perfectly against my silk panties.

I'm briefly aware that three different men have touched these very lucky panties in the last twenty-four hours. Apparently, the normal sex life I'd hoped for is setting the bar too low. Somehow, I've fallen into the option of an extraordinary sex life and there's no going back now.

If sex was an Olympic sport, I'd be going for gold with #1 printed across the ass of these lucky panties of mine.

He pulls back from me just as his hips rock into mine, and heavy breath fans between us just before he quickly speaks like it's the most urgent thing he's ever said. "Did Kais get you off?"

"I—" My pathetic little voice trails away as I shake my head no. I can't believe I'm ready to jump his dick, but I can't actually talk about it. My body and my smutty mind have been ready for this moment for years, but articulating the dirty thoughts seems to be too much for me.

He stills completely. "Has anyone ever gotten you off, Cupcake? Anyone ever whipped your cream?"

"Please, never say that again."

That sexy smile tips his lips again.

"I can go soft if you need it. Go slow. Hard. I can be

whatever you need, Madison. Just tell me." His low rasping tone is like sex itself.

Once again, my lips part, but no filthy words slip out, and nervous thoughts start to drift through my mind, forcing anxiety to press into this perfect moment.

I wanted this so badly, and now it's here and I can't stop thinking. Oh no, what if I end up like Konstance, thinking the female orgasm is a myth, because I can't shut my mind off long enough to let Lighton make me feel good?

That's the thing though. Lighton cares about making me feel good. He cares about me.

What about my future husband?

Deep amber eyes search over my face, following the furrowing of my brow and the downturn pull of my lips.

"What's wrong?" He hovers so close, keeping his mouth close to mine like he might claim it again at any moment.

"What if…" I breathe out the pent up tension in my chest and force myself to ask the ridiculous question that might ruin this perfect moment. "What if once I'm…*blissfully* married, the King doesn't care enough about me to get me off? What if I'm completely miserable for the rest of my life?"

"That's impossible. Women like you don't sit down and let life pass them by." He licks his lips, his gaze slipping down to my mouth again. "As for the King, don't ever depend on a man to take care of you like that."

My eyebrows pull together even harder. Lighton phrases things in the most unique and bewildering way. Even when he's sober.

His mouth stays in that perfect white smile of his, but he shifts, sitting up against the headboard once again and leaving me confused and alone at his side.

"Come here." He lifts his hands, and I sit up slowly. He watches me with quiet attention, and the moment I kneel at his side, he grips my hips and pulls me down onto his lap so I'm straddling him. Big hands clasp low on my hips, skimming over my ass as he adjusts me until my core is firmly against the thick outline beneath his jeans.

"That feel good?" he asks in a low rumbling tone.

I lick my lips and nod.

"Good. Now make it feel even better."

My mouth stays parted, stunned and unsure why this feels like a test right now.

All I wanted was for Lighton to fuck me. Now I'm doing this pass/fail dry fucking that's making me way too anxious to even focus on how good his cock feels against me.

My vagina really is broken.

"What feels good for you?" I finally ask, settling my palms against his strong shoulders.

"Don't worry about what feels good for me. Make yourself feel good, Madison, and I promise if it feels good for you, it'll feel fucking amazing for me."

I nod slowly, and his hands grab me hard, forcing me to grind back and forth against his dick. He stops controlling me the moment my lashes flutter closed. Then I'm riding him, pressing myself against him just right until the rough feel of his jeans and the hard outline of his cock slide so perfectly against the silk material of my panties. My breath catches when his cock grinds against my clit just right.

His hips barely move; he lets me use him just how I want. And I take everything I never knew I needed. His beard scrapes against my skin just before he seals his lips to the low curve of my throat, sucking lightly and then raking his teeth there hard. The palms of his hands slip under my shirt, blazing a path along my ribs before covering my breasts through my bra, squeezing hard, kneading with both palms.

Everything he does is strictly for my pleasure. He wants me to come more than I do, I think, but all I can think about is how many layers separate his skin from mine.

"Take off your shirt."

I fumble between us, and he stiffens as I start to push the button of his jeans aside.

"Madison, it kills me to say this, but I can't fuck you." His voice is pained, his eyebrows tensing like it's the worst thing he's ever had to tell anyone.

Five minutes ago, he was grinding my pussy against his dick, and now he's remembering my virtue?

I hate my hymen right now. I never thought that's something I'd say, but here we fucking are.

"Well, you can still…make me come."

I'm suddenly able to vocalize all the dirty thoughts in my head now that his dick is against my core. It's like my sex drive has found my voice box and is now using it as a mega phone to signal Lighton to a direct path to my orgasm.

He coughs hard, his eyes widening as a slow smile pulls across his lips. "Yeah. I'll make you come as much as you want, Cupcake. It'd literally be my pleasure."

I stand abruptly, and when I shove my panties down my thighs, his lips part, his eyes heating.

"I can't fuck you." He says it like it's just now sinking in. "I can't. I can't fuck you. *Fuck*. I can't fuck you." His head tilts back, banging against the headboard loud enough to make it shake. Frustration lines his face when he looks at me once again. "Come here." He pushes his jeans and black boxer briefs down in a quick

rush and reaches for me.

The hard length of his dick arches up toward his stomach, and I'm suddenly all too aware of how innocent my body is despite my dirty mind. I stand frozen in my spot, my thighs shifting, urging me forward. It isn't until I look up into his sweet brown eyes that I finally take a step forward. Warmth slides over my arm as his gentle touch pulls me closer. He's patient and in control the entire time. If he's anxious like I am, he doesn't show it.

It's like he's done this a thousand times.

He's over six feet tall with waffle abs, for fucking sexy's sake. He probably has done this a thousand times.

Why did I just think that?

My sex drive flips my logical mind the bird because we don't need that kind of negativity in our life right now.

When I settle above him, his palms skim slowly up my thighs, over my bare hips, along my ribs, and he doesn't stop until he slips my shirt all the way off. He leans forward, bringing me nice and close, his hands slipping up my spine, and just like that, he steals away the last article of clothing that separated his body from mine. The bra falls to the floor. The hard planes of his chest skim against my nipples. He keeps his gaze locked on mine, watching me carefully. When I lower my slickness against his cock, he brushes his lips against mine.

Slowly I slide my sex against his shaft, grinding over him just as I had before, but it feels a thousand times better with his bare skin against mine. I feel every rigid part of him against the most sensitive part of me.

"That feel good?" he asks on a groan.

I nod, my breath shuttering out on a gasp.

"Good. Now make it feel even better." His lips slam hard onto mine, and the gentle way he kissed me before isn't anything like the fervent way his mouth is moving against mine now. His tongue demands mine, and I moan against him as my hips start to rock faster and harder against his.

The rough feel of his beard abrades my skin before his lips press a path down my throat. His hips flex just slightly at first as if he still doesn't want to interfere in me using him. But the longer I slide my wetness against him, the more he thrusts to meet my clit just right.

It isn't enough. I want more. I want him filling me completely. But I'll take what he can give me. I'll take every part that Lighton is willing to give.

And fuck is he a giver.

"Lighton." His name is a breathy, thoughtless whisper that forces from my throat, making him groan against my neck. My nails dig into his skin, holding him to me because he's the only thing I have in this entire world when it starts to tremble. My body, my lashes, my world as I know it, shakes as my first orgasm spirals through me.

My pace slows, and his hips no longer thrust against me as I hold myself above him, clinging to his neck and looking down on the most beautiful amber eyes. He watches me with a hooded gaze for several seconds before his lips seal to mine, kissing me with so much desire, so much passion, so much care.

My hand slips between us, and he groans when my palm glides down his thick shaft in one long stroke. He pulls back, peering down at his cock held loosely in my hand.

"You don't have to do that." He barely gets the words out when his eyes close as my palm rubs over the slick head of his dick before sliding back down just to repeat the motion all over again.

It's the sexiest feeling to be in control of his every shaking breath right now. I quicken my pace, and the groan that rumbles through his chest turns me on even more. The harder he gets, the

more I ache to feel him deep inside. His fingers wrap through my hair, and he pulls my lips down to his, kissing me like he knows exactly what I'm thinking right now.

Or maybe he's just thinking the same thing.

Another deep groan hums against my tongue, and he stills against me just as warmth slips down the back of my fingers. A pulsing feeling throbs through his length in my hand.

Our gazes meet, sated and affectionate.

I've never experienced something so intimate with anyone before. For several moments, I stay there in his arms, naked but feeling completely safe and taken care of.

He smiles at me slowly, and before I even realize what he's doing, he wipes my hand clean with Kais's shirt and then wipes himself clean with that same shirt.

Kais's going to be even more pissed than usual when he finds that shirt...and Lighton's come.

But my virtue is intact.

And that's the important thing, isn't it?

Chapter Twenty-Four

Lighton

*I*n exactly one hour, I'm going to have to sneak out of this bed to meet the Elder. And to avoid the fuck out of Kais. I'll have to evade Kais like I didn't rub my dick all over his No Touching Madison Rule Book and make it come and then watch shamefully while it jerked me off.

Should be easy enough.

Just pretend like nothing happened.

Simple.

Her back arches, rocking her ass against me and making me question my self-restraint all over again.

Simple. Easy peasy lemon I'm-going-to-fuck-Madison-Torrent-even-if-it-costs-me-my-dick-itself squeezy.

My arms tighten around her, and the breathy sigh she gives in her sleep makes me rock hard in an instant. I bury my nose in her thick red hair. A sweet scent clings to her locks, and

I realize while I'm doing all this pretending in front of Kais, it'll be very real for me when I have to deal with my memories alone. Madison wrapped me up in her arms and didn't judge me for a single thing I told her.

When I sneak out of this bed and stand there in front of her and all the people I have to pretend for, I won't have her affection to support my shitty, shitty choices in life.

I'll fuck up. It's what I do. It's what I'm painfully good at.

Hell, I'm making mental reports on the girl who just jerked me off. I'll turn those reports in later today to the Elder and maybe it won't be today and maybe it won't be tomorrow, but she'll hate me eventually when she finds out.

A heavy sigh escapes my lips.

I have no idea how to fix the screwed-up mess I'm in. Elder Liddell wants Alice. The misinformed lies I keep feeding him about Madison is confusing him enough for the moment but I know he won't wait around forever.

And I'll keep fucking everything up in the meantime.

I can't believe she trusted me this morning to show me the most vulnerable part of her. Fuck, she's pure.

Good.

Innocent.

Perfect.

And I'm just the asshole who's going to screw all this up for her.

I tense, slowly pulling my arm from beneath her. I sit up with so much carefulness the bed barely moves.

But she knows.

She pulls me back down, my back hitting the mattress flat just before she rolls her naked body onto mine. "Don't go," she mumbles against my chest.

It's not just her naked curves or the way I can feel the heat of her pussy against my side. My heart stumbles from her words alone.

No one's ever wanted me the way Madison does. For over a year now, I've never made an excuse for who I've become. But I've also never had anyone stand up for me and want the person I've become to stick around.

My palm skims up her smooth arm, and my lips press to her forehead. Her breaths even out once more and maybe I won't go. Maybe I'll lie here in the nude and greet Kais with a wave of my cock and just see how he takes the news from there.

Or maybe I'll keep my balls intact and sneak out of here before the angry rabbit gets home.

A flash of movement has me nearly jumping right out of the bed. The pounding feel of my heartbeat urges me to take action, and I grab the lamp off the table and wield it like a baseball bat at the intruder standing in the bedroom doorway.

"Relax. Just checking on my dear sweet sister-in-law. I did expect her to be a bit less naked, but I can't say I'm disappointed." Rotter rakes his gaze all over Madison, and I manage to pull the sheet across her body while still holding the lamp. With my dick out.

Doesn't feel nearly as threatening as it should when he glances from the lamp to my cock and then back again with a bored expression.

Of all the people Wanderlust accepted, it had to accept this murdering fuck. I have to admit, there aren't a lot of people I respect, and there are even fewer people I hate. When a lying sack of shit murders your friends for the fun of it, you tend to hate them.

"Get out." I growl the words, and it's my tone alone that

seems to wake Madison.

She peers up at me before looking back slowly at the man leaning casually against the wall.

"Why are you here, Alixx?" Her hands hold the tattered white sheet over her breasts as she looks up at the deadly man. He takes his time walking over before settling down in the arm chair at our side.

Alixx. She uses his name like he's a person instead of a bloodhound for the King.

"We have a date today, you and I. Oh, and our betrothed. Those two will be there too, I suppose. Tell me, does the King know you're fucking like rabbits in his most trusted advisor's home?"

"I'm not fucking anyone," she says, narrowing her eyes on the murdering psychopath.

"That's a shame. You really should. Don't waste yourself by saving yourself, Alice." He steeples his fingers, the sneer on his lips on prominent display.

He's good. He's good at making everyone around him hate him.

Including the woman he saved just yesterday.

"I'm not wasting myself, and I'm not saving myself, Alixx."

"Why don't you call him Rotter? He's a fucking murderer. Don't feel the need to treat him with respect. He clearly doesn't have any for anyone else." My jaw hurts from how tightly I'm clenching it, and my anger just seems to make him even happier.

"Actually, I'm an assassin."

"What's the difference?" The hate in my tone grows stronger by the second.

"An exchange of money, of course. Otherwise, it'd just be a hobby." He lifts his hands in explanation, and his attention drifts when he realizes I'm still pointing the lamp at him like a loaded gun. "Besides," he adds, "I like when she calls me Alixx. Don't ruin a good thing, *Spy*." He says that nickname very pointedly.

The lamp in my hand dips with surprise, but I level it right back out.

How does he know about that?

"I wish there was just one morning that I could wake up and not be surrounded by craziness, you know?" Madison looks from me to Rotter, and for once, he and I share an equally confused look. She crawls from the bed and wraps the sheet securely around herself before leaving Rotter and me alone while she roams around upstairs, probably looking for something to wear.

I'll just be here with our guest. Casually naked.

"You really didn't fuck her? Not everyone can get the job done. Don't feel bad." He doesn't look at me. He acts like he doesn't care at all for the topic he brought up.

Everything Rotter says is a trap. And I fall face fucking first into it.

"I can get the job done just fine. Madison happens to think I'm above average actually." I don't know why I just said that like he can't see it for himself right now or why I felt the need to verbally rub my cock in his face.

"I've seen better." Rotter shrugs, and it shouldn't make me as crazy as it does, but he's the second person this week who's said that.

Why does everyone keep saying that to me?

"And, she is a slender girl," he says. "Hundred and forty pounds at the most. I bet a grain of rice looks like a mouthful to her." He nods to himself, and it takes me two seconds too long to realize he just compared my junk to a fucking grain of rice.

I stand slowly, and I don't even know what I intend to do. Have a weird cock duel with this fucker just to prove myself?

Because I'd win.

Luckily things don't make it that far. Madison slinks down the stairs in a tight black dress. It hugs her slim frame and pushes up her breasts while leaving miles of her long legs on display.

"You look sinful this morning." Alixx gets this look in his eyes, and I've never in my life seen the prick look genuinely interested in anyone or anything before. He holds his fucking arm out for her, and when she takes it, this caveman part of me wants to rip his limbs off just so he never has another opportunity to hold her hand again.

"Have fun," I blurt instead, smiling like a jackass the entire time.

Madison pauses, her head tilting just slightly like she knows everything about me. She slips out of Rotter's reach, and her small hands press to my chest before she leans forward and brushes her lips against mine. My fingers tangle through her hair, turning the fiery red locks back to blonde once again. I hold her to me, deepening the kiss until my cock is shamelessly hard again in a room full of one too many people.

It shouldn't feel like I'm marking my territory.

But I fucking am.

I bite her lip just before I pull away, and the gasp she gives makes me want to kiss her all over again.

"Thanks, Light," she whispers strangely. "Thanks for this morning." Big green eyes look up at me with so much lust.

A half-smile pulls at my lips because I don't think any girl has ever thanked me for getting them off before.

Damn, she really is sweet.

And then that sweet girl walks off with the deadliest man in the entire Kingdom.

Chapter Twenty-Five

Madison

We spent the early morning and into the afternoon touring the nicest parts of the Kingdom of Wanderlust.

There weren't many. The lane of shops that runs through the center of the village was the nicest part, and we lingered there for hours. It wasn't much. But the King did spend time with me. And his sister. And Alixx.

It's a bizarre relationship the four of us have together, and I don't think it's going to get any easier in the years to come. The entire day has been exhausting with the constant companionship the twins have together. It's tiring to try to keep up and be a part of. But this is the final stop. A speech on the far side of the Kingdom in a clearing in the forest is the very last thing for today, and I couldn't be happier.

The name Alice is a chanting song that attacks me with every step I take. The villagers surround the King's high standing

podium, and he keeps his hand held firmly in mine to show a sense of unity and pride: he did bring his people their Alice after all.

"Alice, Alice, Alice." Over and over and over again that name is thrown at me, and I smile through it all.

Alixx and Konstance stand at my side, just a few feet from the podium, not touching even the slightest bit. I keep glancing at him, and he never once looks at me. He gives adoring glances to his betrothed and even she smiles sweetly at him, which surprises me. Each second they don't threaten to spit in each other's faces is astounding.

"She's here, good people of Wanderlust," Constantine finally calls out, silencing the thousands of people standing before me. There are more of them than I thought there'd be. They're painful to look at. Since I've been here, I've sewn maybe a dozen shirts for this Kingdom.

It's not enough.

They're a sea of tattered clothes and gaunt faces. Big hopeful eyes and a mess of dirty hair.

My stomach sinks and twists just looking out at them.

How can Constantine smile right now?

How can any of these people smile knowing they can't live a healthy life in this Kingdom?

"You trusted my sister and me as your Elders of Wanderlust, and we will take care of you." My head turns to Constantine, confusion washing over my face. *The Elders of Wanderlust.* He doesn't notice me but carries on. "Our Kingdom will progress now. Our future is finally here, and Alice Liddell is going to fix all of our lives."

How? No one has said how I'm going to do that, and when I get home tonight, Kais is going to map this shit out, get me a fucking agenda with a manual and a goddamn handbook with vivid details on how the hell Alice Liddell is supposed to fix this.

"An engagement party will be held for close friends and family, and the ceremony will proceed the following day."

I swallow back a bit of vomit stinging my throat and give the most awful form of a tense smile.

"And then, as you all know, our lives will change. Alice Liddell has arrived. And so has our future."

Cheers erupt, echoing into the night for hours after the four of us walk off that podium.

They're still cheering and saying that name when Constantine tells me he needs to get Konstance home. She apparently has a severe migraine, and her brother must attend to her.

"Kais will take you home." Constantine gently holds my hand in his, and he hasn't once mentioned the engagement party he told his Kingdom about. Or the wedding. Or how I'm supposed to really unite two fucking Kingdoms.

I smile. That's my part to play, isn't it? The smiling idiot who's going to get us all killed.

If so, I'm nailing it.

Constantine leans into me, and I tilt my head up to him, wondering if our first kiss will ever live up to the expectations Lighton has set for me now.

His mouth is tense against my cheek when he brushes his lips there for the briefest of moments. I tense, and he releases me without a second glance, taking his sister's hand and leading her to their shining red carriage.

"Love you too, sweetheart," Alixx calls after Konstance.

Her lips thin, her shoulders stiffening so hard she visibly shakes, but she doesn't acknowledge her betrothed or his snide remark.

"Guess it's just you and me, Alice." Alixx slides his arm

around my shoulder, and I eye his hand when he squeezes me against his side.

Kais's narrowed gaze assesses the two of us for all of half a second before shoving Alixx off of me.

"Ah, yes. Just the two of us," Alixx whispers, striding away, drifting into the crowd. Really, I think he's just testing the people here to see how fast they'll part and dart away from the man who no one ever touches.

"That one's got a few screws loose as well. The men here aren't the most stable, if you haven't noticed." Cat sways toward me.

Tonight, her sheer black dress meets a deep pink corset that matches her hair which is piled high in big curls. Brody's top hat isn't even tall enough to compete with her wave of locks.

Kais storms off after Alixx, and Brody peers back at Cat before he too follows after the men. Cat's bright eyes linger on Brody's back as he leaves. It's a considering look. A sexual look.

"Are you and Brody together?" I lean back on the side of the stage, but Cat starts to climb the wooden beams that are holding up a "Queen Alice" banner. A big splashing red heart is behind the words, and I cringe when I think about the mess I've made of the whole Alice situation.

The goal was to marry the King though, make the Kingdom believe their savior has arrived.

For once, it isn't a mess, I suppose. For once, everything is going according to plan.

The plan just sucks.

"No. Brody wishes. Sometimes I wish too. He's just…not the type."

"The type?" I follow after her, carefully lining up my heels with the wooden rungs. The wind catches my hair, and I'm certain

193

the few villagers who are lingering tonight are getting a full view of the glorious Alice's ass.

"He's just like Kais and just like Lighton. Just like all the men here. None of them have time aside from the rebellion to really give the effort I need. I want romance. I want cuddling, and most of all, I want sex. A lot. All the time." *Preach.* If we weren't climbing aimlessly, I'd give my spirit animal friend a high five right now. "And I'm not settling to be a forgotten woman in their life. I've seen Brody do it to other women, and I refuse to be forgotten." She pulls herself up and takes a seat on the thick beam, letting her legs hang carelessly off the side. Her chin tips up, and I can see how frustrated this conversation makes her.

She's gorgeous. She could have any man in this Kingdom.

But the look in her eyes right now, I know she wants Brody. She's just afraid of having him. She's afraid of being pushed aside.

Is it really easier to never have something than to have something and to let it go?

It doesn't look like it. It looks just as painful. Just as heartbreaking.

She blinks the look away and stares out at the dark horizon. The moon is a full white circle shining down on us. Miles and miles of shady pine trees peek up into the starry night sky. Among all that darkness, a single golden dot shines in the distance.

"What's out there?" I point to the pinprick of light standing alone in the distance.

"That's the Elders' Kingdom." Cat crosses her ankles and gets comfortable at my side. "Before there was Wanderlust, there was Wonderland. Wonderland's a beautiful Kingdom. The land there is thriving and taking care of the Elders." Cat's voice is cutting, tinged with a bit of anger.

"Why wouldn't the King take his people back there? Work

something out with the Elders somehow. They're clearly lacking food here."

"Well, they make up for all their lack of food by eating the plants that relax them, makes them more accepting of their dire situation."

"Is he drugging them? Is Constantine drugging his Kingdom?" My lips part, my voice shaking just slightly.

"We're all just trying to survive," she whispers. "Profit says an Elder made all of this possible. He wanted newcomers. The other Elders didn't." The more she tells me, the harder it becomes to process what I've actually signed up for here. "The other Elders agreed the newcomers could stay, but they didn't want them in their Kingdom. So, they pushed us to the shore with the only two Elders who were willing to stay with us."

"The twins."

She nods quietly.

Maybe Constantine is a good guy. Or he was. Once.

"The one who made this all possible, he wants Alice. The King has faith that by showing a marriage between the most important newcomer and an Elder like himself will create peace and unity between the two Kingdoms."

That's it. It's that easy.

I guess all that I have to do to help these people is be happy. It should be simple.

I can be happy with Constantine.

And his sister.

And Alixx.

I can be happy without Lighton. Or Kais.

…Or Alixx.

Why is this so hard?

Preston, the *Sixth Sense* creeping omen that he is, pops in at my side, and I nearly fall to my death right off the beam that I never should have climbed up on.

"Kais found the come-stained shirt he loaned you. Was it come-stained *before* or *after* he loaned it is the only thing I don't understand. Seems rude to give a lady such a nasty gift, but it's been a while since I dated, so I don't know." His eyes shine when he smiles at me, my pulse barely climbing back down from its near heart attack.

"I don't have money for you. Stop Profit whispering." My arms fold, a heavy sigh slipping from my lips.

"Rotter said he'd foot your bill from now on." Preston leans back, settling in at my side like he's ready to start racking up an invoice for Rotter right here, right now.

I can't believe Alixx would pay this kid off for me.

It's both sweet and…stupid.

"That wasn't a smart thing for him to do, was it?"

"Nope." The kid pops the *p* at the end of that word and tilts his head toward me.

"Get on with it then. Whisper your ominous little whispers about my mother."

I steel my spine as he takes a deep breath and word vomits my past and future out. "Your father never looked for you after he left; you'll never be ordinary despite how much you strive to be; you'll be crowned Queen, but it won't be as pleasant as the King described; the King will find out; several recklessly stupid men will fight to protect you. Oh, and you'll lose your virginity to the least likely candidate."

Wait, what's that last bit about my virginity?

"The King will find out?" Cat shoots a look over to the boy who's now staring aloofly at the stars.

"I can't expand. I tell you all that I know. I only see fragments here and there. The afterlife, that's another story entirely. It's an abundance of information. I can't get some ghosts to go away, and others don't want to be bothered. They're odd entities."

My father didn't look for me? Never? Not once?

I can't be told all the terrible things that await me in my future or in my past or in the afterlife. I thought I could, but I can't. I just can't handle it all.

The board beneath me feels smaller when I stand on my three-inch heels and try to make my way past Preston. He looks confused when I abruptly start to climb down. The breath in my lungs shakes nearly as much as my hands, and I have to really focus on the wooden rungs that are supporting my fumbling body. Halfway down, my heel catches; I gasp when my leg slips, my hands gripping hard but ultimately slipping away from the beam entirely.

I fall the several feet, my eyes clenching closed hard, and I suddenly hope it hurts. I hope I'm knocked unconscious. I hope all of this fades away to blackness just long enough for me to catch my breath again.

Strong arms wrap around me, pulling me against a warm chest. I refuse to open my eyes, but I know who it is just by the adamant way he keeps me flush against him. His breath fans along the column of my neck, his lips coming closer by the second.

"I've never been a savior in my entire life until I met you, Alice. Stop painting me in such a good light, or people will start to think I'm a nice guy," Alixx whispers in a low rasping tone against my ear.

I swallow the thick lump in my throat, and I push away from him on stumbling legs. My dress has ridden up against my thighs, my hair tangled, my palms stinging from the climb.

The assassin and the traitor stand side by side watching the mess that I make everywhere I go.

197

It's then that I realize, I've made friends with the deadliest men of Wanderlust; a spy, a traitor, and a murderer.

And I might be worse than they are.

Because at least they know they're bad. I'm the *good* one. The *sweet* one.

The fucking fake.

When I look up, I meet those tragically beautiful eyes of Kais's. I can't bring myself to believe he's as dangerous as Alixx says he is. I admired the honesty in his eyes when we first met. I thought he'd tell me anything as long as I asked. I thought everything would turn out alright with him guiding me.

I don't know if that's true anymore.

"You can do this, Madison," he says so quietly I barely hear him.

"Things are already more peaceful, just by you being here," Lighton comes forward from the darkness, coming close and making me feel just slightly like I'm among friends instead of colleagues. "Over the years, the King's assassin, who I won't name directly," he pauses to glare over at Alixx. Alixx smirks at him, and it just fuels the tension between the three men. "The King's assassin has been hired to eliminate the rebels. But also, over the years, more and more commoners have become rebels. They're tired of waiting. Simply by being here, by being Alice, you're saving them. How many people have you killed since Madison arrived?" Lighton looks to Rotter, and the man folds his arms over his chest as his eerie smile grows.

"That's confidential information. It doesn't get shared with men who hold no value in this world."

The tension between them snaps.

Lighton's strike is so fast I barely see it. His fist lands with a heavy cracking sound against Alixx's jaw. Every muscle in

his body is tight, his chest rising and falling at a rapid pace as he watches Alixx shake the blow away. A smile curves his bloody lips, revealing crimson-stained teeth and humming laughter. It's like he enjoys the pain.

"Still confidential," Alixx says through that manic amusement.

"There's only been the one on that first night she arrived." Kais shoves himself between the two men, but their hatred toward each other is still right there on the surface. "The King used to dispose of rebels by the dozens. Every day. A peace has settled. The people, the rebels, the King, they all believe what Profit said. Even if you're not the actual person he said it about. You can amend the two Kingdoms."

A sigh slips from my lips, and I wrap my arms around myself harder.

"In my defense, I give the rebels a choice. They can stop rebelling at any time."

"Or die," I finish for him.

"Exactly." Alixx nods happily, not noticing the disgust in my voice.

They're all terrible. Including the King. All of these men I'm surrounding myself with, they're terrible men making terrible choices in a terrible situation.

And I'm going to marry one of them.

Chapter Twenty-Six

Kais

She's thrown herself into a mess of fabric, hiding away in the attic for the last three days. Tomorrow is her engagement party. And this weekend is her wedding.

And the woman pretending to be the soon-to-be happy bride is hiding away from all of it.

I stand quietly watching her from the doorway, studying the focus in her gaze. The little light of the machine shines against her pale green eyes, and she narrows them intently on her work, her hands moving the shimmering fabric quickly beneath the drilling pace of the needle.

"Wear something white to the party. Cast yourself in that innocent image."

"It'll definitely be white." Her voice clips the words out in a sort of mocking tone.

Sometimes I think she hates speaking to me. She trusts me. I can tell she does. But we just don't fit together. It shouldn't

be this hard to talk to the most beautiful, frustrating, ridiculous woman I've ever met.

And if it's so painful to simply talk to her, why do I torture myself by always wanting to be around her?

I can't help but come closer to her. There are warning tones blazing through her voice, telling me to fuck off, and here I am creeping closer.

I didn't expect her to be thanking me. We've all thrown ourselves into this dangerous, shitty situation. But she's the one giving up the most.

She's giving up what her life could have been. Just to save these people she doesn't know.

"Why did you say yes? When I asked you to be Alice, why'd you say yes?"

The steady rhythm of the needle halts, stealing the sound away from the room until only tense silence settles in its place. She considers the question, the corners of her lips pulling down little by little until a real frown is in place.

"I said yes because it sounded like a dream compared to my old life." She glances back at me, and it hurts me to look at her lately. Her long red hair hangs down the center of her back, big green eyes trusting me so damn much when she and I both know she shouldn't. She's beautiful and pure. And all that perfection is going to rot away over the years from being married to a man who won't love her like she should be.

But I understand her answer. Wanderlust feels that way for everyone. Compared to the battlefield I'd left, Wanderlust felt like an absolute fucking dream.

Until it turned dark.

I was here when we left the original Kingdom to come closer to In Trance Island. This realm really was a dream.

At one time.

"What was your life like before?" I lean my hip against her chair, watching her closely, wanting to know everything I can about her before the light in her eyes vanishes.

The King will steal all the beauty of this woman away.

And I hate myself for arranging all of this.

"I had cancer. Twice."

A pain shoots through my heart, and I don't even consciously notice when my hand pushes through her hair. I don't notice until I'm kneeling down in front of her, letting her soft hair tangle through my fingers, forcing her big eyes to look at me.

"How old are you, Madison?"

"Twenty." She breathes out the single word, and her breath skims over my lips.

More guilt washes over me, drowning my thoughts. She's barely even lived.

"What was your life like before you came here?" she asks.

I can't look away from her, and I can see she's taking the focus away from herself and pinning it on me.

Or maybe she truly wants to know who I was.

"I was a soldier."

"And?"

"And that was it. I didn't know how to cope when the war ended. I'm apparently not very good at just being a regular person."

Now she's searching my eyes, and I'm suddenly trying to avoid her gaze. I'm terrified she'll look through me. If she looks inside and finds out I'm just a recovering addict living in a drug addicted world and trying to survive it all, will her trust in me fade?

At first the drugs were meant to help me, heal my broken

leg after the war.

It's strange how something so innocent can turn so dark sometimes.

"Sometimes I have to go to the surface to find the new-comers who are reluctant to find Wanderlust. They're the ones who belong here but keep being deterred. Some come blindly like Lighton, and some, like you, get lost without guidance. So, I go to the surface world to guide them here. No matter how many times I go back, I never feel like I belong there."

Several tension building seconds pass, and I think I said too much. I shouldn't have said all that. Why the fuck did I just tell her that?

"Me neither," she finally says with a small smile that confuses my heartbeat into this stuttering pounding. It hurts when I make her happy even. How twisted is that? "I didn't fit in when I wasn't the Sick Girl. And then I didn't fit in when I was again. I took some time off. I traveled around a lot after high school, but I was still the same. I guess I just felt lost before Wanderlust."

She turns to me, brushing her knee against my arm, making me realize I'm still cupping her face and now her thighs are open to me, and I'm inches away from making another mistake again.

I swallow hard and pull my hands away from her. I stay knelt there, keeping a safe sort of distance between us.

"What was it like before everyone came here? When you were the first, what was it like?"

"Before I came here, things were mundane. Quiet. That's how Constantine described it. The night I arrived, he said that's when it all happened. Time stopped. At first, they didn't notice it. No one did, but their aging process halted, and they noticed after a good long while. More people like me came through In Trance Island every day. It was as if I set something off, but no one ever directly blamed me. They just didn't want me or anyone else messing up their perfect little Kingdom. So they exiled us."

Her eyebrows arch, and I note the red tint to them, making me wonder if the King has noticed as well.

Doubtful. He'd have to glance at her from time to time to notice.

I swallow back the guilt that constantly rises in me when I think of Madison and the fucking relationship I threw her into.

"You're not the white rabbit," is all she finally says.

"What?"

"You're Time. As in a person. The one who halts time because of the Hatter. Oh my God, I trusted you because you were the humble rabbit, and you were Time all along? In some stories, you're the villain. I trusted the villain." Her voice raises, and I have absolutely no idea what's causing the terrified look in her eyes or what the hell she's talking about.

I go to speak, but she stands abruptly and starts pacing around the room, letting the fabric hanging from the ceiling brush over her shoulders as she walks a long line from one side of the room to the other.

"If I'm the Hatter—*the Hattress*—I'm going to anger you."

"What do you mean, Madison?" I stand, but she doesn't stop her back and forth walking, barely looking my way at all while she seems to think all this through.

"In the book, time halts in Wonderland because the Hatter angers Time. As in a person. As in you. I'm going to do something that angers you. Like the wrath of Time. It all makes sense now. You make sense. Time is dependable but uncontrollable. Very touchy." She eyes me up and down with a knowing nod and I feel insulted from the look alone but I have no idea why.

Lighton walks up the stairs, and it just seems to set her

rambling off even more.

"And you…no, you're definitely the March Hare. Never mind." She nods her head, but none of it makes any more sense to me than it did before.

Trying to understand Madison Torrent is like trying to read a book.

In Latin.

During the middle of a hurricane.

On a life raft.

That's sinking.

"Who's Alixx?" she asks as if she hasn't met the assassin a dozen times.

"What the hell is going on right now?" I grind out the question, but neither one of them even notices.

"He's probably one of those mindless cards running around following orders without a head of their own to think with," Lighton says, and my gaze narrows on him when he walks right up to Madison, his hand drifting absently to her hip, stopping her in her tracks until she's forced to look up to him. He grounds her with a single touch.

What. The. Fuck.

"Stop touching her like a lover would." That little statement seems to get their attention.

"Stop trying to make ship happen." Madison slips away from Lighton, but his eyes follow her every move.

Literally the more she speaks, the more I don't understand.

"Ship? Is that like a millennial thing I hear when I'm in the surface world? Is this like ratchet? Or fleek. Tea. Is this one of those weird word things again, because I can't. I can't do another word that's not a real word. Sorry. *Not sorry*." I add the last little part, and it makes her smile.

"You sound like the cool grandpa at the retirement center right now." Lighton smirks at me.

"And stop bunching several generations into the millennial category every time something new happens that you don't like, Grandpa." Madison rolls her eyes, and now I'm definitely insulted.

Lighton finally shows the smallest hint of seriousness and explains. "She's talking about Wonderland the book. And ship is a book thing meaning you're trying to make a relationship with two people who don't actually have a relationship. Like me and Cupcake over here. No relationship for us. Two completely separate people. You know she's engaged even? To the King. You'd have to be an idiot to try something with the King's betrothed." He lifts his hands at his sides like he's an open fucking book, and the subtle glance Madison gives him tells me he's lying.

Lighton is definitely the idiot who would try something with the King's betrothed.

"This isn't a book. Our lives are not storybooks. Start acting like this is all real life." My growling tone shows my irritation, and it makes Madison's smile fall.

It's always my tone.

"Yes. This is definitely not a book. Because you"—she points an accusing finger at me, coming close until only a few inches separate us—"you have the sharp jawline of a perfect book boyfriend. Bad boy tattoos. Smoldering eyes." My heart does that ridiculous stumble it always does when she's near, but this time, hearing her say all the things she likes about me, it's so much worse. And better. And worse all at the same time. "But the writers completely fucked up your personality, Kais."

That settles my heartbeat. Pushes it right back down into a manageable pace as she walks away from both Lighton and myself.

Leaving us stunned like the two biggest idiots who are just stupid enough to have it bad for the King's betrothed.

Chapter Twenty-Seven

Madison

Tonight, it all becomes real. Tonight, I'm accepting my place as Alice Liddell, attending an official engagement party, and tomorrow, I'll marry the King. I'll be a Queen, and my whole damn life will be the fairy tale young girls have been spoon-fed their entire lives.

Sounds kind of extreme for a girl who just wanted ordinary.

"You ready?" Kais asks.

He stops dead in his tracks when I turn around.

The sheer white fabric covers nearly every inch of my skin, shimmering over my body, clinging to me like water coating my flesh. It dips into a deep *V* and ties in a pretty bow at the side. And only a few precautious parts of me are not on display beneath the see through, virginal white dress.

I can't help but love to piss off Kais by following his orders.

"That—that is definitely the color of innocence," Lighton says on a throaty whisper.

"I can see your breasts, and why the fuck are you wearing red panties?" Kais grinds out.

"Do you want me to take them off?" I cock my head to one side, and only Lighton seems to find me amusing right now.

Seriously though, if the fate of this realm really rests on the color of my panties then the Kingdom is more fragile than I realized.

"I think you're spending too much time with Rotter. You're starting to sound like him now." Kais pushes his hand down his face and gives me another long, *hard* look.

I can't help but notice both of them as well. Kais's black tuxedo covers his arms, highlighting the black ink that slinks down his knuckles and along his throat. Number 4884 is nicely in red, sneaking out above his crisp white collar.

He's so dangerously attractive.

And Lighton…

"You shaved." I don't know why I say it like a man shaving is the most awe-inspiring thing I've ever witnessed in my life, but he looks so different. He looks…sleek. Responsible. Mature.

Sexy.

"I thought I'd clean-up for the wedding." His eyes become too serious, and that single word changes the mood in the room.

My wedding.

Right.

"Ready?" Kais nods toward the stairs, and I don't move for a few seconds even as I start to nod.

"Yeah." Still I don't move.

Kais's steps are slow, pressing evenly against the wooden

floorboards until he stands in front of me. His warm hand slides down over the sheer sleeve of the dress, and he takes my hand in his. He fully slides his fingers through mine without hesitation. The pure blue of his eyes shines like the edge of a knife. There's something dangerous and cutting in his gaze like he could slice me wide open with a single look and see everything I'm hiding inside. He's this odd combination of violent strength and alarming gentleness. The gentle, caring side of him surprises me every time a glimpse is shown.

"I'm sorry for what I put you through for you to get here." His eyes search mine, and I realize this is the second time he's apologized. I both love and hate that he's apologizing. He gets an alarmingly gentle look in his deadly gaze when he's sincere. I only ever see it when he's like this with me. "I'm sorry, Madison."

I want to wrap my arms around him and never let him go. He's strong and kind and…not mine.

Not at all.

"Will you two still be with me after tomorrow?" The tremble of my words makes a pain crack through my chest. Emotions sneak up on me all at once, and I'm holding my breath just for their answer.

Don't leave me alone.

Don't leave me.

Lighton comes to me, drawn to me it seems, and he doesn't stop until his fingers slide into my free hand, surrounding me with the two men I never expected to care about.

"I think I still owe you orgasms, and I don't like to leave a debt in my name, so I'll definitely be sneaking into the castle for a while," Lighton whispers against my hair, earning him a stern glare from the other man at my side. Lighton's gaze shifts from me to Kais and the nonexistent space between us. "People who live in glass houses shouldn't get stoned, my friend," he says with a cocky smirk.

Kais shakes his head, rolling his eyes the entire time. "You've been clean for a week now. You just say this shit to piss me off."

"I have no idea what you're talking about." Light keeps his features vacant as he shrugs, and I honestly don't know if he really does do it on purpose or not.

And I don't care.

Because I really do care too much for the worst men in this Kingdom.

Including one I should have listened to right from the start.

I never should have touched Alixx Stone.

He reminds me of just that the moment I arrive at the party.

His fingers run the full length of my spine, barely slipping away when he reaches the low curve of my back. He lets the secret touch linger before walking fully away. "Classy dress," he says over his shoulder, a cruel smile perched on his lips as he strides toward the drink table.

Leaving me...alone.

Lighton and Kais keep a healthy distance a few yards away, keeping mostly to themselves while Kais watches the crowd closely. The guy really knows how to bring a party down. If someone so much as stares at me for too long, they're met with a death glare that Satan himself would scurry away from.

I roll my eyes, and a puff of air slips from my lips.

You know who I haven't seen? Not once.

Constantine.

Or even his sister for that matter.

I dwell on the fact that I'm alone at my engagement party as I study the ballroom. I haven't been in this part of the castle yet, but we walked through the entrance throne room to get here. Two white doors shine under the golden chandelier lights above, and I keep glancing at that exit repeatedly.

I could leave…

They could all toast to the soon-to-be bride and groom without us, right?

Preston slips in by my side.

I guess I'm not completely alone.

"That guy, San Antonio, the guy you tried to lose your virginity to never gets laid again, if that makes you feel better," Preston whispers, taking a long drink of what appears to be scotch.

I bite my lip.

That does weirdly make me feel better. I'm glad Fort Worth didn't get the chance to put another girl through another thirty second hip fucking ever again.

"Would I have died? In the surface world, would I have died?"

He nods and downs the rest of his drink.

"Everyone dies. What kind of waste of psychic power is that question?"

"I meant of cancer. Would I have died of cancer if I stayed?"

"Oh, yeah. You would have died. Would have been a sad funeral too because, as you and I both know, you're shit at making friends."

"Thanks, Preston. I needed that confidence boost."

"That's what I'm here for." He shrugs and pulls a silver

flask from the inside of his coat pocket.

A hand slips into mine, a warm breath slides along my throat for the briefest of seconds. "Come with me." And then Alixx pulls me away.

A popping sound cracks through my skull, making me wince, and when my eyes open, we're in a dark hall. His hands push down my hips, and he guides me in place until he seems happy with my position.

"What are you doing?" I hiss, but he covers my mouth with his hand.

I struggle against him, my elbow jarring back into his ribs, but he doesn't make a single sound of discomfort, if anything he seems to enjoy the way my body struggles and fights against his. He lets me fight him for several seconds, quiet laughter shaking manically through his chest before he slowly lifts his other hand and points at the small hole in the wall.

My arms lower, my curiosity outweighing my annoyance for just a moment.

When I peer into the stream of light, looking quietly through the wall, I see the most astounding thing. It happens so fast. Constantine slams into her from behind. The King's thrusting stops as quickly as it started, and the girl doesn't make a sound as she lowers her silk skirt back into place. He tucks himself away, and I note that he's breathing heavy and she's not. She's barely even wrinkled her clothes, which is depressing in itself.

Disgust twists through my stomach at the thought of watching them have sex while I stand here in secrecy with Alixx.

"Do they have a relationship outside of this?" My whisper echoes around the empty hall.

"Other than this twenty second interaction every single day, no." Alixx's breath heats my neck as his chest brushes closer against my back, keeping his right hand poised along my jaw

and then my throat, along my collar bone. A tingling sensation spreads through me, and I force myself not to lean into him.

His touch is addicting. He touches me the way no one ever has. It's not even sexual. It's like he wants to feel me, wants to know what every inch of my skin feels like against his.

"So it's not likely they'll continue fucking after I'm crowned queen," I say, trying not to let my voice tremble from the way he's skimming his fingers down my shoulder blade.

I can hear the cutting amusement in his tone before he even speaks. "Well, no, once you're queen, he won't need her. Once he has you, you'll get the honor of being Twenty Second Tina."

My lips thin at his snarky remark, and I turn to him in the darkness.

"That's not even her name, you made that up."

I can see the sparkle of amusement in his bright eyes as he looks down at me, tilting his head close, letting his breath fan across my skin. He's so close I can't take it that he's not touching me now. I physically ache for his hands to return to me. Maybe this was his way of conditioning me. In a twisted way, I know he wants me to crave his touch.

Just like he craves mine.

My palm lifts between us, and he watches the hesitant way my hand slides up his chest. The quiet breath leaving his lips stops, forgotten in his lungs while he simply lives off the way my fingers are drifting across his hard body.

"Why'd you show me this, Alixx?"

Was it to hurt me?

Oddly I'm not hurt. I don't know why, but I can't bring myself to be astounded that the man I'm about to marry just fucked Twenty Second Tina.

"Everything Constantine does is routine without much thought. Because he's lived for so long it's hard to find happiness in the mundane." He pauses and the way he says it makes me wonder if he's actually talking about Constantine at all. "Lust is mundane to him. I did it to show you the ugly inside the good." His hands whisper down my sides, brushing along my skin so lightly that I feel his touch like blazing fire through the thin material of my dress. "Absolutely nothing in this world is as kind or as good or as pure as it seems. Our King included. You included. Me included."

"No offense, but I don't think anyone's ever called you any of those things, Alixx." My chin tips up to him. Of all the times that I've pushed away from him, pushed out of his arms, here I am leaning into him until my chest is firmly against his.

"That's where you're wrong. I was once a very…charming man. A long, long time ago. I'm not anymore. But I am honest. With you. You and I are setting out to live terrible lives. In a way, that makes us friends."

"Friends is a bit of a stretch. Allies is more like it."

His lips skim against my jaw before brushing over the shell of my ear with the heat of his whispered words. "We have common interests, keeping secrets and telling lies." The smile I feel curving along his mouth shouldn't make me smirk like a lunatic, but I am. "We bond together. Enjoy spending time together." He pulls me harder to him until I can feel the thick outline beneath his slacks against my lower stomach.

"I can't think of a single time I enjoyed spending time with you, Alixx." My words say one thing while my roaming hands slipping down his defined shoulders say another.

"You're not enjoying this right now?" His palms push over my breasts, squeezing them and making desire bloom right through my core in so much tingling energy that I gasp a startled breath against his neck. And the bastard is right there waiting

when my body melds against his.

But I refuse to admit what he wants.

"Not one bit," I whisper on a heavy breath.

His laughter is a knowing, condescending sound. His teeth nip at my ear, and I've never felt aching tension like the energy that's sparking all around me, consuming me until it's all I feel deep inside.

"Sometimes I think I like you better as an enemy, Madison. It feels rewardingly bad, dirty even, to know I'm helping a traitor, to *want* the traitor. I crave that twisted feeling of shame, and I think deep down, you do too." His index finger trails down my ribs before he fists my dress, and I feel the hem start to rise as he inch by inch pulls it slowly up. He pulls back just enough to feel my breath against his lips, his eyes shining with dissecting curiosity as he watches me while I wait for the feel of his hand to shift just a little lower. The dress lifts all the way to my hip, and he grips the material tightly in his hand before trailing his index finger ever so slowly along the smooth inner curve of my thigh. His touch is so faint I barely feel it when he trails down the center of my silk panties, down, down, down until he's cupping my sex, finding my truth within my lies. And I know he knows then. Because I feel my wetness against his touch.

Just like he does.

"Or maybe I'm wrong, and we're just two strangers who hate each other as much as you say." A crackling sound follows his words, and then light burns into my eyes. The quiet darkness is stolen away from us, and the bright light of the throne room and the ramble of voices and laughter from the adjoining room falls into its place.

And then, Alixx Stone releases his hold on me and walks away. He adjusts his tie and the lapels of his seemingly tailor-made jacket that falls so perfectly around his wings. He strides toward the white double doors of the ballroom as if nothing just happened.

I'm left breathing heavily and trying to understand why I feel like I just lost something I never really had. I can pretend to be confused all I want, but I know why.

I don't want to be fucked and forgotten like that woman in the King's room. I don't want that to be my future. Even if tomorrow it will be.

Right now, I want something real. For once in my life, I want something normal and extraordinary all at the same time. I want the bad and the good.

I want Alixx.

"Wait." His back stiffens, his suit pulling tight against his broad shoulders.

He turns to me with that mask of unfazed amusement, but I see the interest in his eyes. It's like lightning in his gaze, lighting up the emptiness of his bright green eyes.

"Come here." I say it with more confidence than I feel. I say it like I'm mimicking the way Lighton said it to me.

And I think it's working.

That easy stride, that "I don't have one fuck to spare," that "I know exactly who I am and where I'm going" attitude of his comes right back to me. I swallow hard when he looks down on me with waiting attention.

It's now or never.

I thought my life started the moment I fell into this mysterious world.

I was wrong. It starts right now.

No more missed opportunities and no more uncertainty.

I am who I am, and Alixx has never made me feel unimportant or overlooked. I've only ever felt confident when he's

around. When he's around, I'm exactly the person I pretend to be.

My hand slips into his, and I lead him the few feet back to the King's throne. It sits right next to the smaller, more delicate Queen's throne. *My throne*. His brow arches up when I push him down in the enormous gold seat. The moment of surprise on his face is short-lived, and he gets comfortable like he's sat in this chair since the day he was born. His elbows settle on the arm rests, and he steeples his fingers in an arrogant way while he quietly watches me with amused interest.

I hold his gaze. I let the moment build, and he lets me, passing his gaze back and forth between my eyes until I grab the pretty bow on my dress and pull.

The sheer fabric wafts around my body before splaying open for him and him alone. A triangle of red material covers my body, and his attention drifts there immediately. My thumbs hook into the waist of my panties, and he follows the path they lead down my hips, thighs and legs before I pull them off. The moment they're in my hand, he leans forward and steals them away, tucking them into the front pocket of his slacks.

My brow lifts, my lips parting without words for a few moments.

"Safe keeping. Don't want anyone to find them forgotten later, Sweet Madison."

I can't help but love when he says my real name. He cruelly taunts Alice's name around me so much that it makes my heart come to life at the simple sound of his sincerity.

I nod to him, my gaze narrowing suspiciously on him before my palms push over his shoulders, and my knees settle on either side of his legs. He pulls me closer, his fingers gripping me painfully as he slides me fully against his erection.

My lashes flutter, but I keep my attention on him. "So, you're going to give them back?"

He shakes his head.

"Not a fucking chance," he whispers against my lips.

He's never once made the move to kiss me. Maybe he's afraid I'd push him away like I always do when he touches me. I can't, for the life of me, imagine him afraid of anything.

But he does seem afraid of me sometimes. Afraid of getting too close despite how close he always keeps me.

His fingers brush down the valley of my breasts, making slow work of trailing over my stomach before slipping down my folds with so much pressure I gasp when he presses hard against my clit. His eyes watch mine, drinking in my every emotion before his fingers slip lower, sinking into me so slowly I have to stifle the moan caught in my throat.

"Mmm, that's right, give me all those innocent sounds, My Sweet Madison." His mouth brushes against the curve of my neck as his fingers arch deep inside me.

My fingers fumble against the button of his slacks, but his other hand settles over mine. "Go slow." His words confuse me, and he seems to see it in my features. "I know you think I'm an asshole, but I'm not a quick fuck. I'm going to make every part of you feel good."

Go slow? We're about to fuck on the King's throne with a hundred people in the next room over, one of whom is said King.

"What if someone comes in?" My voice shakes, and the weak sound of it only makes his pace quicken, slamming into me so hard another moan slips out.

"They'll turn around and walk right back out. Don't think about those other people. Right now, you're mine." My heart stumbles when he says that. He places a careful kiss to the side of my jaw, his lips coming closer and stopping right at the corner of my mouth.

I turn to him, and he stills when I lean forward. His body holds pure tension until my lips press slowly to his. Every angry word I've ever said to him and every wanting thing I've never spoken is pressed into the passion of that kiss. His tongue meets mine like we're both starving to taste each other, and all that control and concern that was just in my mind is torn away as I start to thrust against his hand. He releases his hold on my wrist to tangle his fingers through my perfectly curled hair. He fists it hard, and he doesn't stop me this time when I start to undo the button of his pants.

The moment my fingers push down the length of his shaft, the urgency of the situation seems to fire through us both. His hips rock against my palm in steady even strokes that match my own, both of us needing the other more than just the sensual touches we're sharing right now. Faster and harder, we work against each other, breathing in one another's quieted, needy sounds.

When it rises too high, when it feels like it's too much, I stop. It's so abrupt it takes him a second to pull back from me, worry lighting his eyes for the very first time since I met him.

He's worried.

About me.

About us.

But he shouldn't be.

I lift myself, steadying myself against the man I love to hate. The one I can't seem to feel anything but trust for. I trust him more than I trust myself right now.

It's easy to hate the villains.

No one ever tells you it's just as easy to fall for them.

His big hands clasp over my hips, and he lines me up until his cock brushes against my slickness. He holds my gaze, he holds me in place, he holds all the control right now as he lowers my hips ever so slowly.

His lashes waver, but he never looks away from me when he fills me slowly inch by inch. A prickle of pain is faintly there, but it's washed away with a blooming feeling of uncontrollable want. My hips rock subtly. When I gasp against his lips, they curve up in the devious smile he always has, but this time it's a lazy smile of pleasure. And something else.

Something dark and dirty.

"That's it. Fuck me like you hate me, Sweet Madison."

Guilt spirals through me in a nasty sensation that makes me want to shove away from him like I always do. Then he kisses me, drowning me in that fucking irrational craving that I reserve just for him. And then I do exactly what he told me to do.

I thrust down on him so hard that both of us moan against one another, my nails clutching into his shoulders, digging into his jacket. I wish his clothes were gone just so I could draw blood and make him feel all the terrible, addicting, and delicious things he always makes me feel.

My teeth sink into his lower lip, not bothering to drag over the skin lightly or teasingly, doing it solely to give him the pain I know he wants.

Blood tinges my mouth just as he groans low and rumbling.

His fingers dig into the curve of my ass, and he holds me down against him, forcing me to take every single inch of him. I struggle to find a rhythm again, shifting in his arms, but he never releases me. It's a controlling hold that I'd momentarily forgotten he was capable of. It feels cruel, but the way he's looking at me isn't. He keeps me held there without a hint of space between us, and I swear I do hate him. I hate him.

And then he grinds his hips up, thrusting up even though there's nowhere to go, but he goes deeper anyway. Firmly he pins

my hips down on his cock, his every move presses against my clit, sending pulsing tingles through my body with every meticulous thrust he gives me.

I relax against him, my body shuddering as my lashes flutter, my cries becoming louder and louder the more he works me. Harder he fucks me with bruising strength, but it isn't enough.

My eyes meet his, and for the first time, there's an honesty to his gaze, an open pureness in the way he's looking at me. He doesn't look like the man everyone fears. He looks like a man who's been hurt, and abandoned, and completely discarded.

My palm lifts to the base of his jaw, my fingers skimming over that long slicing scar that leads all the way up his face. His attention flickers over my curiosity during our moment of innocent intimacy.

And then he tips his head back and pushes his throat harder into my palm.

I gasp when he slides ever so slowly out of me and then forcefully back in. It's a delicious mixture of sweet darkness.

Just like Alixx.

It takes me only a moment to understand what he wants. My index finger tenses just slightly over his skin, and a heavy breath of air shakes from his lips, making me understand him on a deeper level with one single breath. My palm flexes, nails biting into his neck with the briefest hint of pain, danger, and blatant arousal.

He pushes into my palm even harder, but this time for another reason. His mouth slams to mine, his tongue sliding over mine in the deepest kiss of my entire life. My grip on him shifts, and I hold him with both hands fisting his inky hair.

Long fingers skim hesitantly over the column of my throat. My heartbeat climbs with every touch he gives me. He lingers there for a single second before sliding his hand carefully away. I can still feel his touch even when his lips brush gently to the side of my neck. I barely feel the light raking of his teeth before he bites there hard enough to make me scream.

And then I come. I tremble violently in his arms, and he growls a pleased sound, releasing his tight hold on my hips and fucking me a bit more recklessly until he too groans into my neck. He stills in an instant, but his lips press sweet, tender kisses over the painful spot on my throat. Hooded eyes study that mark on my neck for several seconds before he kisses there once more. His hands push up and down my spine, and he holds me so gently to him like I'm the most valuable thing this demented man has ever had in his life.

Moments pass before he unfolds a white pocket square from his suit jacket. I watch him in confusion when he pushes it along his split lip. He stares down at the small tinge of blood for several seconds before folding the napkin neatly into quarters and pushing it into his pocket as if saving it for another time.

When his dangerously beautiful eyes look up at me, he shows me a vulnerable little hint in his gaze. It's a slightly worried look like I might judge him for something, judge him the way the rest of the world judges him.

Or maybe…he's afraid.

My palm shakes when I bring it up to the sharp angle of his jaw. His head tilts, leaning into my touch just slightly. He and I are like two thrown out pieces of completely different puzzles that somehow fit side by misplaced side.

My lips skim against his, and I think that one sweet, chaste kiss tells him all the things I never say to him. As much as I hate him, I also want him.

Until he speaks.

"Come along, Sweet Sister. We mustn't keep your fiancé waiting."

Chapter Twenty-Eight

Madison

The following morning is like a blur, and when Cat hands me a glass of Rosen, I down it in one big drink. Her pink eyebrows arch, and she flags one of the many women rushing around to get me another two to three glasses of Rosen.

"You're doing fine," she says with a cat-like smile that does absolutely nothing for my nerves.

A white dress taunts me from a hook that it's hung upon across the tent that I'm getting ready in. Fucking white dress. Fucking wedding. Fucking Alixx and his fucking perfect fucking.

It was exactly what I wanted: sex filled with passion and desire. And now I'll never have it again. After the delicious soreness of my body fades, it'll be like last night never happened.

If I'd just had boring, unwanted sex with Constantine for the rest of my life, I'd never know what I was missing.

And now I know, and now I want that and so much more.

I want that so bad that it hurts.

The angry breath that shoves out of my lungs sounds more anxious than furious, and Cat just thrusts another glass of Rosen in my hands. I take it just like I did the last.

When she pulls my hair back to start curling it, she stops dead in her tracks.

"Oh." She coughs, and a sly smile pulls wide across her lips. "That sexy bruise on your neck is going to require some make-up for today. And tomorrow. And the next day." She winks at me with a sultry smile.

My eyes widen. I grab the hand-held sterling silver mirror to take a better look at the horrible assaulting bruise.

All I can do is cringe.

And so does Kais when he walks inside my tent.

He turns on his heels with murderous intent in his sky blue eyes and swings that glare to Lighton who stumbles into the other man.

"What?" Lighton takes a step back from the violent look that says he'll murder Lighton for even glancing my way right now.

"Did you fucking fuck her?" Kais grabs Lighton by his neatly pressed collar and hauls him off the ground. "We had one fucking rule. One!"

"He didn't!" I screech.

The few women in the tent pretend to be busying themselves with fanning out my dress that seems to be getting whiter with each passing second.

"Leave," Kais doesn't even look their way, and the women scurry out the moment he speaks. He releases Lighton and spins on me, giving me the full effect of his dangerous gaze. He swallows, soothing the aggression in him before he brings his attention back to me with a bit more control. "Did you fuck Lighton?" he

asks in a very calm, collected tone.

"No," I growl out.

The tent wafts open, and the last person who should walk in here right now strides right in.

"Miss me?" Alixx's smile is pure sin and bad decisions.

And Kais sees it right from the start.

The twitching of his jaw is the only premeditated sign of what's about to happen. Kais's fist comes up in a show of unrepressed strength. A thud of breathlessness leaves Alixx as he doubles over against Kais's fist that's still settled firmly into the man's abdomen.

"You fucking touched her when you knew how important she is. You selfish fuck." Kais shoves Alixx off of him, throwing him to the tent floor and glaring down on him even as Alixx gives him that fuck you smile.

"You really think she's as innocent as you keep telling her she is?" Alixx's laugh turns maniacal as he pushes himself off the ground with one hand. "Did it ever occur to you—"

I cut off his nasty words before he says something that will get him killed. "I fucked him. I…I wanted…I just…it's my fault." My voice grows incredibly small, and the only people who aren't glaring at me right now are Cat and Alixx. Who are both smiling like I made the world's best decision, and I hate them both for how much encouraging approval they're giving me in this moment.

"Why?" Lighton blurts like it's the only logical question. "Why Rotter? Was I not around? Could you not find me? I was there."

Fuck. My. Life.

I didn't think Alixx's smile could be any more wolfish, but watching me try to explain to Lighton why I fucked Alixx, instead of either of the two men standing before me, turns his manic smile into a slashing display of perfect white teeth as he slowly gets to his feet again.

"I—"

"I'm going to deal with this after the wedding," Kais tells Alixx as calmly as possible. His agitation comes back to life within seconds though. "I hope fucking her is worth a war." There's barely any distance between the two men as he glares hard into Alixx's eyes.

There's one single second when he looks at me and something flashes in the assassin's eyes.

Sadness? Guilt? Both?

But when he turns back to Kais, it's gone. The look reflected in Alixx's gaze is cruel amusement now. "It was just one ally helping another. It was meaningless, really. Just one meaningless moment in a lifetime of meaningless moments."

Pain sinks through me slowly. It's a different kind of pain that sears and spreads in my chest. It's nothing like any hurt I've ever felt in my life and I hate that he caused it so easily.

And I hate that I let him cause it.

Meaningless. That defining title, that's what hurts the most. It has me dissecting every single moment I've ever spent with him.

We tell everyone around us thousands of lies. Was what he just said a lie for Kais, or were all the things he's said before a lie for me?

I thought we were allies. And then I thought we were friends.

The truth is, we're nothing.

Just two people in a miserable situation that can only get worse.

And I'm just now seeing that.

"She has a wedding to prepare for. All three of you need to leave. Now." Cat stands, pressing her long fingers to her hips in a power pose of irrefutable dominance. She's petite, beautiful, and currently telling three of Wanderlust's most dangerous men to get the fuck out.

Alixx looks away with that disgustingly arrogant smile still tilting his lips. He takes a moment to adjust his tie and crisp white cuff links. He glances from Cat to me. His attention holds on me for so long it makes my stomach knot. I hate the way he's looking at me.

I thought I knew that look.

He exits without a word to me.

Kais never looks away from me, and it makes me fidget under his gaze. The fierce tattooed man has a lot of worry in his eyes right now.

He walks the few feet toward me and leans over my chair, wrapping me up in that scent of his that gives me the strangest feeling that everything will be alright as long as he's near.

"Be careful," he whispers, his breath fanning along my neck. He pulls back, his gaze locked on mine even as he walks away.

Lighton passes me a long look. He doesn't move an inch. He doesn't say a word, and I think that hurts more than if he'd screamed in my face.

He turns to walk out.

"Wait." I rush over to him, letting the morning sunlight warm my face as it sneaks inside. My heart hurts, and I don't know what to say or do or even if I should touch him or not. I've never felt so unsure around him.

"You don't have to say anything. You're about to get married, and I'm being ridiculous." He shakes his head, and the laughter that he breathes out is so forced it cuts off abruptly.

His golden hair is combed back neatly. Big brown eyes shine down on me, and he looks so different from when I first met him. He's sober.

And hurting.

I hurt him even more than he already was.

"I'm sorry." My hand slips into his because I just can't stand not touching him.

He searches my eyes slowly. Then he leans in, the sunlight cutting across his bronze skin, and then he presses his lips to mine. He kisses me on my wedding day like he's the only man I should ever kiss for the rest of my life.

His tongue flicks against mine, making me arch into him before he pulls slowly away, making me chase the taste of his lips. He tilts his head, his five o'clock shadow brushing along my ear. He whispers so quietly I barely hear his rasping words, "Do you want me?" My eyes never open, but I nod to him, feeling like my heart's going to break at any minute today. "Do you want Rotter?"

That pain burns in my heart like it'll never leave for the rest of my life.

Fuck Rotter.

My jaw clenches and I shake my head hard even though it feels like a lie that I never even spoke.

"That's all I need to know," he whispers.

He kisses me again, pressing my back into a thin wooden beam supporting the tent, making the structure shake from the force of his kiss. The kiss is so rushed, so needy, so fervent, I'm sure he'll fuck me right here. His hips rock against mine just once, making me feel the hard outline of his erection before he steps abruptly back. Heavy breaths shake out of him, and he watches me as I hold myself up on that little flimsy support beam. He watches me like

he's trying to remember me just as I am.

He opens the tent but pauses there. "You're a beautiful bride, by the way."

"My hair's a wreck, I don't have makeup on, and my dress is still on its hanger." I smile softly, but the smile doesn't stay.

"Then I meant you look sexy with your lips all swollen from my kiss. Is that better?" The smirk he passes me is the last thing I see before he walks away.

I don't feel any better. But I don't feel any worse either.

I exhale the pent-up breath, and just before I turn away, someone else walks in.

Will this day never end?

Konstance stands before me and, in her satin flats, she and I are the same height. And she's also wearing white. The exact same white in the exact same wedding dress.

Oh my fucking twin obsession.

"Hi," she smiles a tight-lipped smile. She's completely ready, looking glamorous and perfect while I stand in my jammies, and all I've done today is watch my friend beat the shit out of her fiancé because he fucked her sister-in-law.

Me.

This wedding's going to be a mess.

This life is going to be a mess.

"Try on the dress; I wanted to make sure we looked perfect today. I thought it'd be a good bonding experience for us to match."

"You picked out our matching dresses? I'm twenty years old, and you bought me a matching dress?"

"Yes, of course. I thought it'd be fun. Something that'd make Constantine happy."

"Yeah." I nod to her, repressing my urge to scream and rip the sweet white dress into a thousand tiny shreds of virginal confetti.

"Okay." Her smile falters just a bit like she's exceeded her friendliness limit for the day. "I'll see you out there." She smooths the front of the white gown, and I glare at the fabric as she walks away.

"We have to hurry. You only have an hour to get ready," Cat says from somewhere behind me.

One hour.

That's plenty of time to make a wedding dress meant for a false Alice.

And that's exactly what I'll do.

Chapter Twenty-Nine

Madison

Okay, I was wrong. One hour is not enough time to make a wedding dress. Not even false Alice would wear the atrocity I came up with. I glare at the tattered tulle that I've cut the dress into that's far too high for a formal gown.

I peer down at my blonde locks that Cat's curled in the time that it's taken me to rip the dress into shreds that's supposed to resemble some kind of dress. I think about the easy way Lighton washes away my red hair so easily. He just skims it with his fingertips.

I trail my palm along the messy fabric.

He takes my red hair and makes it blonde. It's simple. It's just a change of colors.

It seems easy. Effortless.

And so it is.

An ink spot bleeds into the center of the gown. It grows

larger and larger until the black chases out the white, and all that's left is a dark, mourning style dress in my hands.

With its messy tulle and tight bodice, it reminds me of the eighties in a way. Meh, I love the eighties. Who doesn't love the eighties? This is a hundred times better than matching a woman who already has a twin. She doesn't need another for tweedle-fuck's sake.

The dress does have a little bit of a funeral vibe but in a good way.

My positivity is unstoppable this morning.

Give me a break, I need irrational positivity.

Cat bites back her smile when I pull on the dress.

"There are sex bruises on your hips," she mutters.

"Shut up, Cat." I smirk back at her, and she comes closer to help me zip up the back of the short dress.

Brody slips in through the cream-colored tent door, and he eyes my black dress with an arched eyebrow. "Konstance has asked again if Alice is ready. Should I tell her you need another minute? Or sixty?"

Cat shoves him and his remark back out of the tent. She stops in her tracks the moment she pushes him away, and then she pulls him right back. He stumbles. His confusion only grows when she steals the black top hat from his head and shoves him right back out.

Delicately she traces the red silk around the base of it before slipping it in place on my head.

I can't help the smile on my face.

I knew I was the Mad Hattress.

Or possibly an eighties rock legend.

Definitely the Hattress, though.

In another five minutes, she pins my hair in big curls that hide my parting gift from Alixx.

Then silence settles in.

"I think you're ready." Her voice is quiet like she doesn't want to say it, and I don't really want her to say it either. "You know you don't have—"

"Ready?" Konstance's voice cuts in, and then it shrieks into a terrible sound of anger. "What are you wearing? That is *not* our dress. What happened to our dress?" She searches the small tent frantically, but I rush past her.

Today is my wedding day. It's my day. It's the fairy tale I've never dreamed of, and it's going to be beautiful.

The wind catches my long blonde hair, and I smooth it down on the one side that matters, and I don't stop running until I see him.

A long stripe of bright red silk lines the grass. It travels past the hundreds of chairs and their seated guests, and there at the end of the aisle, at the edge of the cliff is the very first person I saw when I entered this realm.

The ocean breeze lifts his pale locks. Numbers in slashing lines of crimson cut across his jawline. Numbers 4884. My numbers.

Kais St. Croix is waiting for me, perfect and handsome like he just stepped out of the crisp ocean breeze itself. And he's standing next to the man I intend to marry.

I take a single step, but then Konstance brushes past me. When she starts to walk the aisle, violins strum to life in a swaying, pure melody. Constantine's eyes shine with affection as he watches his sister walk toward him. I linger there, watching the two of them, my gaze searching the hundreds of people until I spot a man watching me intently.

Alixx leans against the side of the castle, a good distance away from everyone else including his bride. The shadows of his dark wings hide his deviously handsome features, the scar cutting across his cheek, and the heated look in his gaze as he watches me, standing here like I might run away from Wanderlust and never look back.

Was this another bad decision? Was accepting Kais's offer to be Alice a mistake? What about befriending Lighton when we both knew we were better off alone? What about seeking out the one man everyone shuns? What about lying to all of these people just to save them?

None of that felt like a mistake. It didn't feel bad when I was doing it. It's a hard line to walk between doing good and bad when there's so much bad to dive into.

But I never dived into any of this. I was pulled in.

I could have been honest and walked away at any time.

I'm not Alice, or the Hatter, or that Sick Girl. I'm Madison Torrent. My future is whatever I make it.

And if I'm Queen, I'll be able to make it exactly what we all need it to be.

In the small crowd of people, my eyes meet Lighton's warm honey gaze for a single second before pulling toward the man waiting for me at the center of the aisle. I lift my head and take a single step onto that beautiful red fabric.

The smallest, politest voice I've ever heard cuts through the enchanting notes of the violins. "Excuse me? I'm terribly sorry to interrupt this lovely wedding, but I seem to be lost."

A woman in a billowing blue dress and golden blonde hair looks up at me with big eyes the color of the sea.

And I know exactly who she is just by the innocent look in her eyes.

Alice Liddell just fucked up all of our plans. As well as my life.

The End.

A Note from the Author

The Villainous Wonderland Series is a reverse harem series. Madison will get her harem of villains. I wanted to restate that in case anyone was worried because I know these characters are incredibly imperfect and it will take them a minute to get their shit together for this harem;)

Thank you so much for reading! Book two, Within the Wonder is now on preorder.

into the maddness

About the Author

A.K. Koonce is a USA Today bestselling author. She's mom by day and a fantasy and paranormal romance writer by night. She keeps her fantastical stories in her mind on an endless loop while she tries her best to focus on her actual life and not that of the spectacular, but demanding, fictional characters who always fill her thoughts.

Printed in Great Britain
by Amazon

81813367R00141